NEW YORK

World-famous magician Doctor Black dazzles a packed house at Carnagie Hall, then suddenly disappears.

MIAMI

Silent eyes glare down at a sinister meeting of faceless conspirators. Nightshade is on the loose.

HAITI

Schizophrenia and a self-destructive quest for vengeance emerge as the legendary Mama Dimanche appears in the Haitian jungle. It's all part of Nightshade's dark debut, a graphic thriller with an introduction by Walter B. (The Shadow) Gibson.

WEIRD HEROES

A NEW AMERICAN PULP™

VOLUME 4
NIGHTSHADE

A NOVEL BY

TAPPAN KING AND **BETH MEACHAM**

Based on a Character by Mark Arnold, Meacham and King

GRAPHICS BY
RUDY NEBRES

EDITOR
BYRON PREISS

PYRAMID BOOKS ▲ NEW YORK

PRODUCED BY
BYRON PREISS VISUAL PUBLICATIONS, INC.

Letters of comment, as usual, are welcomed. Please address mail to WEIRD
HEROES c/o Byron Preiss Visual Publications, Inc., 680 Fifth Ave., N.Y., N.Y.
10019. The next WEIRD HEROES, Doc Phoenix, will be available in January. A
novel by Ted White and Marv Wolfson, more fantastic art by Stephen Fabian.

Pyramid Edition published October, 1976

"The stories, characters, and incidents mentioned in this book are
entirely fictional. No actual persons, living or dead, are intended or
should be inferred."

ISBN: 0-515-04035-5

Library of Congress Catalog Card Number: 76-41106

Printed in the United States of America

WEIRD HEROES, A New American Pulp is a trademark of
Byron Preiss Visual Publications, Inc.

Typography and Production by Anthony Basile

Cover Painting by Ralph Reese

All art produced especially for WEIRD HEROES. This is the first publication of a novel featuring NIGHTSHADE/DOCTOR BLACK.

We are privileged to present this new introduction by
the dean of American pulp writers and, not incidently,
one of the oldest living and most respected magicians
in the world. Colleague of Houdini, author of the
Shadow, this piece by Walter Gibson is a rare, Weird
Heroes treasure.

THE
SHADOW
SPEAKS!

AN INTRODUCTION BY
WALTER B. GIBSON

As an avid follower of detective mysteries over a
stretch of some seventy years, I can recall the high
points that caused decided changes in popular trends
because they caught the spirit of their times and
thereby captured the mass market of that particular
day, while providing a nostalgic touch that is con-
tinually with us.

I remember riding in Hansom cabs in Philadelphia at
the very time when I was reading about Sherlock Holmes
doing the same thing in London. True, he and Dr. Wat-
son were usually racing to Paddington to catch an express that would convey them to some distant scene of
rural crime, while I was merely accompanying my mother
to Broad Street Station to take a local train to our
suburban home following a Christmas shopping trip;
but the settings were similar and each seemed equally
real. I was learning at an early age that if you could
identify yourself with a scene or situation, your imagination would practically place you there. As
proof, the readership of the Holmes stories spread
like an epidemic and when imitators sprang up from
every quarter, it didn't disturb good old Sherlock.
Instead of being en-gulfed by the tidal wave, he came
riding along on the crest.

I realize now that Sherlock Holmes epitomized our
way of life as it was befor World War I. The changes

wrought by that conflict demanded a complete turn-about in crime-writing styles to reach the general populace. It was provided in the person of that insidious villain, Dr. Fu Manchu. Though his inception came earlier when he was but one of various villains concocted by Sax Rohmer, and it was not until the League of Nations began to totter with threats of another world-wide conflict that the insidious doctor reached his peak, playing upon the growing fears of readers at large.

Fu Manchu responded to the tensions of the international scene, but in the American arena, there were other pressing problems. The gang wars of the Prohibition era, the poverty and injustices brought on by the depression, the speed with which criminals could move in motor vehicles, the threatened breakdown of society itself, all provided an opening for a character who could right such wrongs and establish the image of a national hero.

It was my good fortune to build up such a character through the adventures of The Shadow, which I penned under the name of Maxwell Grant all during the 1930s and the 1940s. For ten of those years, The Shadow novels appeared twice a month, which was proof both of their popularity and the fact that they were really needed. The fact that the Hero Era had arrived to stay a while was proven by the troupe that followed in The Shadow's wake. They included The Phantom, The Spider, Doc Savage, The Whisperer, Operator Five, Secret Agent X, The Avenger and even a revival of Nick Carter, a popular sleuth of the Sherlock Holmes vintage.

Since The Shadow was launched on an experimental basis, there was only one way to maintain its popularity and that was to keep it attuned to the spirit of the times. The readers wanted a hero, so in their eyes, The Shadow remained a hero and those who stood with him on the side of right were given their share of his reflected glory. Always, there was a distinct line between good and bad where the characters were concerned (though at the outset, some were left undefined to keep the reader guessing until a late chapter).

The readers wanted it that way because they thought that way and the line of demarcation was continued on through World War II, until The Shadow Magazine finally suspended publication a few years later, several years after the other magazines had folded. Further evidence of this policy is found in the Hero Comics which continued through the years that followed, for analysts of pulp and comic magazines have all but unanimously agreed that The Shadow triggered the trend.

The reissue of The Shadow novels in paperback form has further stressed this point. Nostalgic readers have recognized anew that no matter how fanciful the stories might become, the descriptions of places and people are accurate in essential details, so that the basic ideas of The Shadow apply to the America of today as well. No matter how complicated some of the plots became, the motivation of the characters remained simple: Good against Bad.

Now nearly thirty years later, we find history repeating itself in cyclic fashion. The first NIGHT-SHADE adventure, TERROR, INC., continues this tradition with a schizophrenic adventuress, Nightshade, as the heroine. It presents realistic characters, living in today's surroundings, meeting issues that mark the spirit of the present times. That, in itself, explains the difference. Where The Shadow's ultimate aim was justice over evil, with any hint of vengeance an impersonal by-p oduct, Nightshade is compelled by vengeance as a prime motivation.

Unlike The Shadow, who had the background of a wartime hero, Nightshade is a victim seeking retribution on the people who victimized her. The Shadow, always cool and calculating, could strike only in the cause of justice, while Nightshade, never totally sane, can act only under the urge of vengeance. Even when The Shadow uncovered crime in high places, it was a sure sign that bad men had supplanted good and taken over an honest enterprise. In today's world, things are more complex, and the "villain" Nightshade fights is not an individual but an entire multimillion-dollar corporation.

Thus both may be fitting, according to their times and their lights. The Shadow, cloaked master in an era where action was regarded as a man's prerogative; Nightshade, a figure of destiny precipitated into a modern world where women are taking a more active part. Regardless of the contrasts: Good versus Bad; Complex versus Simple; Justice versus Vengeance, one fact stands paramount:

The spirit of the "pulps" or "character stories" as we often termed them, still is riding high. May Nightshade long continue to uphold the tradition of The Shadow.

—Walter B. Gibson
August, 1976

A WORD FROM THE EDITOR

A book of firsts, this fourth volume of WEIRD HEROES. First book illustrations by Rudy Nebres, noted illustrator of Kung Fu and adventure graphic stories for Marvel; first words from Walter Gibson for this new American pulp; and, more significantly, first publication of TERROR, INC. The premiere Nightshade novel by Beth Meacham and Tappan King.

I won't divulge much about the character herself (themselves, as you'll see) or about how she developed. That task is admirably done by the authors in their afterword. Instead, I will take my space for speaking about Nightshade and the series, and the rather curious relationship between them.

WEIRD HEROES exists as an alternative home for heroic action. Its heroes for the most part exist in our present or near-future time. To validly call itself a NEW American pulp, our concept and approach to the heroic theme is hopefully an evolution of what has gone before. Our main intent is to provide entertaining adventure fiction in which the main characters solve their problems in some other way than violence. Alternative problem solving or a pretentious effort at redirecting a genre, whatever you call it, WH is new.

NIGHTSHADE at first glance (or glare) might appear to be a contradiction of goals. There's a stereotypical organization out to take over the world and a heroine who has vowed to fight them. There is tragedy, blood is spilled in the name of vengeance, and a woman named Mama Dimanche makes her way to the front of a revolution.

Yet there is so much more that is only glimpsed at in this premiere. For NIGHTSHADE is a complicated creature. Her lust will consume her, her past compels her and her present, which you are about to experience, is an obsessive nightmare half-way to and from defeat. Nightshade's actions drive her closer to a dark goal, but, as her confidant and mentor Clara Weiss perceives, it is not the path to peace.

In the context of WEIRD HEROES, this is a grimmer tale than most. The hero of the title is actually an anti-hero and we pity her rather than cheer her ahead.

It is a thriller, with feminism, stage magic and espionage weaving a complex background to a mysterious game. Beth Meacham, Tappan King and Mark Arnold have strived to provide an entertaining and realistic adventure. Together with Rudy Nebres' sweeping art, it is a convincing debut for a dark and surprising character. Her destiny may not be what you think.

Byron Preiss, New York, N.Y,

MAGIC AND MADNESS!
NIGHTSHADE

BOOK ONE
TERROR, INC.

The judge should not
be young; he should
have learned to know
evil, not from his
own soul, but from late and
long observation of
the nature of evil
in others: knowledge
should be his
guide, not personal
experience.

Plato,
The Republic
Book III.

1

PROMINENT EXEC DEAD AT 53
NEW YORK—Henry M. Southern,
President of Daneco Corp., died of an
apparent heart attack yesterday mor-
ning in the Executive Offices of World
Transport Enterprises, Inc.

He is survived by his wife, Elizabeth,
and two children. Memorial services

Henry Southern was late for an important meeting with a
man he had never met. Waiting impatiently for the express elevator to the 86th floor of the World Transport
Enterprises' massive glass-faced building, he mopped his
brow, straightened his tie, and tried to remember the
man's name. Wilson . . . ? Wilkins . . . ? He shook his

head as the empty elevator opened, and stepped in, bracing for the acceleration. The doors closed.

* * *

Margo Jansen, a temp who staffed the front desk during lunch hour, looked up as the bell for the express elevator signalled its arrival at the 86th floor. The door opened, and Margo stiffened with shock. A man lay crumpled on the elevator floor. Ignoring the insistent buzz of the telephone, she rushed to stop the doors from squeezing shut.

Bracing the door with her hip, she rolled the man's face over. He was dead. She turned away from him to call for help and noticed a spot of blood on her sleeve where she had cradled his head.

* * *

Elizabeth Southern was the epitome of an executive's wife. Elegant, sophisticated and poised, she dealt efficiently with the brutal fact of her husband's death, just as she had efficiently maintained his life for him.

Now, facing her first night alone, she wept. She crushed a handkerchief against her mouth and fought to control her grief, but each time she did, another memory of her life with Henry would rise up, and tears would begin again. Any thought of the future without Henry was unthinkable.

Along with grief, she felt a colder emotion: a combination of fear and futile rage. The doctors of World Transport were curt and emphatic: her husband suffered a heart attack. She had accepted the diagnosis quietly, but she could not make herself believe it. She sat, weeping in the darkened apartment, feeling the burden of her helplessness crush down upon her—until at last, a shrill sound pierced through her numb despair. She realized the telephone had been ringing for some time. Summoning her strength, she reached for the receiver.

"Yes?"

"Mrs. Southern, I am—a friend. I've just learned of your husband's tragic death, and I would like to help you."

Elizabeth Southern heard in the caller's words a hint of something dark—something which touched the heart of her own fears.

"Do you know something about . . . Henry's death?"

"I would very much like to discuss it with you. I think we can be of assistance to one another."

Elizabeth Southern felt a surge of hope at the woman's words. "I—if only you *could* help me—I—I can't . . ."

"I understand, Mrs. Southern. Are you free this evening?"

"This evening?"

"Yes. That is, if it would not be too trying for you to speak about your husband's death so soon afterward."

For some reason she could not explain, Elizabeth Southern trusted her anonymous caller. She sounded so sure, so confident—a person she could unburden her fears to. Shaking herself, she said, "I think—I would like to talk to someone about it."

"Good. Tonight, then?"

Elizabeth Southern became silent in the darkness, alone.

"Mrs. Southern?"

"Yes—yes, tonight. Where shall I meet you?"

* * *

The sky was darkening as Margo Jansen returned home with a bag of groceries. She walked up the three flights to her apartment. Quickly disengaging the series of locks which protected her small room and few possessions, she deposited the bag on the table in the

15

kitchen alcove. It had been a difficult day, and Margo was glad to be home.

As she crossed to the light switch, a woman's voice spoke from the darkness in a deep and vibrant whisper.

"*Do not turn on the light.*"

Margo froze. In the dim light of the street lamps, she could make out the figure of a tall woman dressed in black. She could see a pale, lean face with gleaming ice-blue eyes above the darkness of the clothes.

"Who—who are you? How did you get in here?"

"*Call me Nightshade.*"

The words shot coldly through Margo Jansen, but she remained unafraid.

The voice continued. "I hoped to find you home, but you were delayed. I let myself in and waited. Do not worry. I will not harm you."

"What do you want?"

The shadowy figure moved closer. "You were present when Henry Southern died."

"I—I had nothing to do with that. It was a heart attack . . ."

"When did you notice the blood on your sleeve?"

"*Blood*? I don't understand . . ."

The woman named Nightshade reached out of the darkness. Her hand chillingly clasped around Margo's wrist. "*Here*, Miss Jansen."

There was a dark smear on Margo's sleeve. She tried to pull away but the grip was firm.

"What do you want from me? Leave me alone!"

Powerful eyes peered deeply into her own. "*I must have your help.*"

Staring into that haunted face, those terrible eyes, Margo realized she would have little choice. "I will do whatever you ask."

* * *

Nightshade moved swiftly across the Manhattan roof-tops, coming finally to the gravel-covered roof of a squat building on the edge of the Village. Lifting a concealed panel, she dropped down into a small darkened room. She donned a pair of dark glasses, and stepped out into the glaring lights of the corridor.

Clara Weiss was completing the last of the day's medical records when she heard faint footsteps. A hand-some woman in her late fifties, Dr. Weiss was lined and white-haired. She hung her white lab coat on a hook in her office, and looked up. Nightshade stood near the door, a brightly colored cloth clutched in one hand.

"There you are, dear," said Clara. "I was beginning to worry about you." She gestured at the cloth Nightshade was holding. "What have you there?"

"This?" Nightshade held up the blouse. "No end in itself, but something that may lead me to *him*."

"I had hoped it was finished." Clara's gentle face hardened.

"No. I was afraid I had lost his track, but now I've found it again. He's there, I can feel it, behind the Southern death. And this will prove it." Nightshade's voice darkened, and her hands tightened. This time he'll pay for what he did."

"So, the hunt begins again." There was bitterness in Clara's voice. "How are you going to use this 'proof' of yours?"

"I have to be sure of it first. I'll be in the laboratory." Nightshade turned away and started down the corridor.

"*Nightshade*."

She turned, her eyes widening at Clara's unaccustomed use of her personal name.

Clara continued, more softly, "I don't suppose you realize how late it is? The work can wait. You have barely an hour to reach the theatre. You wouldn't want to be late for Lili Black's opening performance."

"Theatre? Oh, of course. I forgot."

"You better go change, dear."

"Yes, Clara. I'll go now."

* * *

Nightshade walked the length of the corridor that joined Clara's clinic office with their brownstone townhouse. She followed a winding stairway to her room, which she entered without turning on the lights, and shut the door behind her.

She sat down before a dressing table and removed her dark glasses, then carefully placed a pair of tinted contact lenses over her sensitive eyes. Only then did she snap on the blazing lights that surrounded the mirror and look at the face reflected there. Nightshade winced at her image. She could still see the fine traces of scar tissue around her nose and mouth, traces that extended down to her neck and chest. The skin on her forehead and around her eyes bore the faint but unmistakable white gloss of healed burns.

She reached for the jars before her. With hands skilled by long experience, she began to disguise the surface of her face. The scars were covered, the angles softened, the eyes and mouth made gentle.

Reaching toward a stand, she selected a wig of rich dark hair that curved softly around her face. She looked up and smiled. The change in her face was complete—she would dress now.

The woman studied the final effect in the harsh light. Pleased with what she saw . . . Lili Black left her room and followed the winding staircase back down to Clara's office.

"Well, how do I look?"

Clara gave an appraising glance as her companion entered, smiling radiantly, dressed in a stylish version of a tuxedo, complete with white tie and tails.

"Stunning. And just in time. I've called a cab. It should be here in a few minutes."

2

What could explain the long lines of people entering Carnegie Hall? Some looked like young circus fans, but it was not a circus. Some were dressed in the bizarre paraphernalia of youth, as if they were rock groups scheduled that night. Many were dressed in the opulent garb of the first-nighters, as if to applaud a flamboyant ballet star or a brash new musical, but no such entertainment was waiting inside. A few wore the rumpled, untidy garb of the intellectual or bohemian and many stars were as plain as the face of New York. In short, a cross-section of a great city had come to the hall in hope of being admitted to the performance of Doctor Black.

The woman who called herself Doctor Black brought the City a new thrill, turning the stale routine of the stage magician into a dazzling new artform . . . She did so with such flair, such enterprise, that the uneasily impressed metropolis had become intoxicated with her.

She stood alone on the stage, illuminated by a single blue-white spot which gave no hint of its origin. Her long hands, her pale face, and the whiter pale of lace at her wrists and neck, gleamed coolly. Only hints of her tall figure and raven hair showed against the blackness of the stage. She spoke in a sudden crisp, clear voice.

"As all of you know, there is no such thing as magic. Everything you will see tonight you will be sure is illusion. Only know this—that there was a time, not so long ago, when forces moved and shaped our lives, forces whose whispers are still heard today. Let us hope there is some suggestion of those days in this simple entertainment."

Doctor Black gestured to the wings. Two young men dressed in black wheeled out a dark wooden square box filled with coarse white gravel. They exited quietly.

"For my first illusion this evening, ladies and gentlemen, I should like to present for your amusement *L'Arbre de la Vie*, 'The Tree of Life,' first said to have been performed by the celebrated French magician Jean-Eugene Robert Houdin."

Her white hands moved with a rapid flourish. Empty only seconds before, they now held a small square silver box.

"This box contains the fabled seed of 'The Tree of Life,' older than time itself, yet capable of growing to maturity in the twinkling of an eye."

The magician took from the box a small sparkling seed. The box vanished with a turn of her wrist. She drew her hand above her head with a commanding gesture, paused, then dashed the seed into the large box.

There was a flash of flame and a crash of cymbals.

"*Voila!*"

From the square of crushed stone drifted a wan tendril of smoke. It swirled and writhed with serpentine life, and a shape began to appear in its midst. An astonished murmur rose up from the audience as the slim sapling, only inches high, crept slowly out of the stone.

"Behold, 'The Tree of Life!'" Her voice sent a thrill through the watching crowd as the shoot began to grow before their eyes. As it pushed its way up, leaves appeared on the tiny limbs. It shimmered silvery, in and out of sight like a phantom, each time appearing taller and fuller. Soon it passed the magician's waist, and she stepped back, beckoning. The swirling mists continued to wreath the tree as it grew.

Finally, with triumphal gesticulation, Doctor Black cast her hands high up, and the spectral tree stood higher than her head. She bowed quickly, and there was a short spontaneous burst of applause. She silenced it with a glance.

"A moment, ladies and gentlemen. If I might have complete silence."

There was quiet. With a snap, her hand darted in a circle and down, and the tree was instantly laden with gleaming silver fruit. Again the audience sounded its approval as the magician plucked a sample from one of the limbs.

With a slight impish gesture, Doctor Black nodded, and the tree flickered and vanished. As she bowed low the unbroken accolade exploded, climbed to a crescendo, then died.

She paused, regarding the silver fruit with a wry smile. The two attendants silently removed the gravel-filled box. She spun quickly, and placed a tripod and burnished brazier waist high before her.

"Thank you. Now I would like to offer as an interlude a few small samples of the conjurer's art. Observe."

She tossed the silver fruit into the brazier. It burst into multicolored flames. She passed her hand through the flames, unharmed. Her fingers spun, and she slowly drew from the fire a long flame-colored silk cloth. She draped the cloth over her closed hand, and began to push it into her fist. Once more, she enclosed the scarf in her fist and withdrew it, this time a pure white. She cupped the silky whiteness in both hands and tossed it high above her head where it took wing, becoming an ivory dove. She gestured again, and the flames turned to blue—a third time, and they became green, from which she drew a green silk. Another move, and there appeared on stage a green parrot. The bird perched on her shoulder as she produced another bird of canary yellow, which lit on her other shoulder. She transferred the birds to one arm, drew yet another crimson silk from the flames, and cast it over them. They vanished. She tossed the silk into the fire where it flared, and the flames died away.

Taking the brazier in one hand, the tripod in the other, the magician whirled again, and turned to face the audience empty handed, bowing. The dazzling rapid-fire productions and disappearances left the crowd delighted.

Again she waited for the tumult to cease.

"You are most kind." She bowed a second time. With a signal, she called her assistants to the stage.

"I shall require for my next illusion the aid of a volunteer." She cast an intense glance into the audience.

"You, sir." She winked and crooked a finger. "Yes, you. I need a big strong man for this presentation."

The man who reluctantly came to the stage was a tall broad-shouldered man in his early thirties. He was dressed in a three-piece suit. He seemed ill at ease.

"Now, then, Mr. . . . ?"

"Russell, Mark Russell."

"Mr. Russell, if you would be so kind as to take this rope . . . ?"

"What rope?"

"I *am* sorry, how careless of me." Suddenly a rope appeared in her hand.

"*This* rope, Mr. Russell." The audience chuckled. "Please take this rope and securely bind my hands behind my back."

She turned slightly away from the hall. The volunteer began to tie a series of knots about her wrists, quickly and tightly.

"Very good, Mr. Russell. You were a boy scout?"

"Navy."

"Of course."

When he had finished, she spoke again.

"Now if you would be so good as to bind my ankles as well . . ."

Russell looked perplexed.

"What is it? Oh! The rope. You'll find it, I believe, in your inside coat pocket."

Russell fumbled in his pocket, then incredulously pulled out another rope. He stood, dumbfounded.

"My ankles, Mr. Russell."

He shook himself, knelt, and began to truss her ankles. When he finished, she looked down as if annoyed.

"Can't you make the knots any tighter? Here, let me help you." She pulled her hands, untied, from behind her back and bent to help him. He nodded, then realized her hands were free and insisted on binding her again. The audience was beginning to laugh out loud.

"Thank you, Mr. Russell. Gentlemen?" The two assistants stepped offstage and returned with a tall silver cabinet on wheels. One opened the front. The interior was black.

"If you will assist the gentlemen . . . ?" The three men lifted the magician and placed her, standing, in the cabinet. The door was closed. From within the cabinet, the magician's voice sounded clearly.

"Mr. Russell, if you please, lift the top section of this cabinet and place it on the stage."

Russell, encouraged by the assistants, walked to the cabinet. He lifted the top third of the cabinet, which separated along a barely perceptible hairline. With some effort, he placed the cube on the stage. From within the small box the magician's voice spoke. Russell pulled back.

"Thank you. Now if you will assist the gentlemen with the other two sections . . . ?" The two in black lifted the center section and placed it to the cabinet's right. From this section now came Doctor Black's voice. "Very good. *Now*, gentlemen."

With Russell's dazed help, they stacked the cubes back in place, in inverted order. There was a pause. The audience began to stir. Finally, there was a distinct tapping from within. The two assistants pulled open the door.

The magician stood, still bound, in the confines of the small cabinet. The assistants, lifting her out, began to unbind her ankles. Russell began the difficult business of undoing the same knots he had so securely tied.

Doctor Black waited patiently while he completed his work. Then, her hands free, she shook his hand. He seemed startled at her touch.

"Thank you *so* much, Mr. Russell. You've been very cooperative. Oh, just one more thing. Did you happen to lose this?"

She handed him his watch. The people guffawed.

"And this . . . ?" She returned his wallet.

"Or perhaps this . . . ?" She returned his vest.

Russell thanked her, and began edging off the stage.

"Oh, Mr. Russell? One last thing." The magician whispered something in his ear, pressing a ball of white cloth into his hand. He turned red, and fled from the stage.

She bowed again, and was greeted with mixed laughter and enthusiastic applause.

Doctor Black gave the embarrassed man time to regain his seat. The bright lights which illuminated the stage dimmed, and again she was centered in the spotlight.

"The feat which I am about to perform has not been attemted on stage for over two decades. First performed over two centuries ago, it has taken the life of virtually every magician who regularly undertook it. This is the only presentation that Houdini himself did not dare perform.

"Ladies and gentlemen, for your entertainment this evening—the Bullet-Catching Trick!"

The magician looked into the front row. In a raised voice she called out: "Captain Curtiss! Your assistance, please."

A burly, middle-aged man rose from the audience, and walked onstage carrying a small black box.

"My guest is Captain Howard Curtiss of the New York Police Department. He has volunteered to remain after the performance for those who wish to verify his credentials. I have been allowed to perform this presentation only on the stipulation that an officer of the law be present. Captain Curtiss, will you tell the audience what you have in the box you are holding?"

"Certainly. This sealed box contains a standard issue police revolver, like those routinely carried by New York City police officers on patrol."

"Thank you. You have examined the gun and verified that it is genuine?"

"Yes, Ma'm. We subjected the weapon to a rigorous series of examinations, including a test firing."

"And your findings?"

We found the weapon to be in perfect working order, and we are satisfied that there has been no tampering with its mechanism."

"Thank you, Captain Curtiss. Now, before we proceed, would you please review, for the benefit of the audience, the request I made of you one week ago?"

"Yes. After you had assured my superior officer that there would be no liability to myself or the force in the event of any—unforeseen circumstances, I was assigned to cooperate fully with your request."

"Which was . . . ?"

"To fire one round of standard ammunition at close range directly at your heart, tonight, on this stage."

"And are you prepared to carry out your assignment?"

"I am."

"Very well. Shall we proceed?"

The magician gestured to her assistants. She walked to the right of the stage, and braced herself against a metal stand prepared for her. Curtiss broke the seal on the box, lifted out the gun, opened the magazine, and loaded a single bullet into it. Laying the weapon across his forearm, he took careful aim. Satisfied, he lowered the weapon.

"At your signal, Ma'm."

Doctor Black turned to the audience. "Again, I must ask that there be complete silence during the presentation. Those of you in the smoking section are requested to extinguish your cigarettes. Please refrain from unnecessary noise, for Captain Curtiss' sake."

The hall fell silent. The magician returned to her position.

"Are you ready, Captain Curtiss?"

"Ready."

"Take aim."

As Curtiss raised the gun again, a voice was heard from offstage. The gun was lowered. As the tension broke, the audience began to murmur. Doctor Black silenced them, as one of her assistants emerged from the wings holding a yellow sheet of paper.

"Your attention, ladies and gentlemen. I have just received a telegram." She crossed the stage with the telegram, and handed it to the police officer.

"Captain Curtiss—would you kindly read the message to the audience?"

The policeman began haltingly.

"It's addressed . to you, Doctor Black, in care of Carnegie Hall—from . . . it's signed 'S.A.M.' "

"The Society of American Magicians—please, go on."

"Doctor Black, Carnegie Hall. 'Respectfully urge you do not attempt Bullet-Catching Trick. Sixteen previous performances resulted in death.' "

The magician was silent a moment, as if in deliberation, then spoke.

"Ladies and gentlemen, while I appreciate the concern of so prestigious an organization as the Society of American Magicians, I consider it my professional responsibility to continue. If there are no further objections . . . ? Captain Curtiss, are you ready?"

"I am."

"Take aim." Again the policeman raised the gun. Doctor Black held a small white kerchief at her hip in readiness.

"At my signal . . ." There was a long, still pause.

"*Fire*!" There was a deafening noise.

Her hand flew up. She staggered back. A woman gasped. The magician began to slump forward, straightened, and held the cloth high above her head with a triumphant flourish, displaying the bullet. The audience exploded.

"A moment, please, ladies and gentlemen. Captain Curtiss, would you examine the contents of my handkerchief?"

They met at midstage. Curtiss took the cloth from her, and opened it in his hand.

"What do you see?"

"It looks like a standard gauge bullet, such as is fired by this gun. It has been flattened, as if in concussion with a hard surface."

"And when would you say it was fired?"

"It would be impossible to determine without tests, but judging by its warmth, and the traces of powder on the handkerchief, I would say it has been fired in the last five minutes."

"Thank you, Captain Curtiss, your cooperation has been greatly appreciated."

As Curtiss returned to his seat, the audience was on its feet, cheering loudly and more insistently. The magician bowed deeply to cries of "bravo" and "encore."

Finally, she raised her hand for silence, smiled faintly, bowed once more, and vanished. Swiftly the lights came up as the curtain fell.

3

Elizabeth Southern stood in the crowded hall at the rear of the stage, waiting for Doctor Black as she stepped from the apron.

"Mrs. Southern?"

She nodded.

"I'm Lili Black."

They clasped hands firmly.

"I must change, Mrs. Southern. I'll only be a moment."

Lili Black stepped into her dressing room, and emerged later, dressed in white linen pants, a cream jersey, a scarf and dark glasses. She took Elizabeth Southern's arm and escorted her to the street, immediately flagging down a cab.

"Tenth and Fifth." Her voice was cold, almost imperious. Then, remembering herself, she turned to her companion, smiling, and said, "I'm glad you could arrange to meet me here, Mrs. Southern."

"Thank you, very much. I'm very grateful you have taken an interest in my problems."

"Not at all. My motives are not entirely unselfish."

* * *

Elizabeth Southern was sure they had walked at least six blocks through Greenwich Village after the taxi halted. It was, however, very dark, and with the twistings and turnings, she lost her sense of direction. All she knew was that she stood before the door of an Edwardian brown—or, more properly—a black-stone house of three stories that faced a garden courtyard. In the glow of two amber carriage-lamps, the number "7" was visible. The black door held a brass knocker in the form of a dragon.

Clara Weiss met them inside. She seemed surprised at the unexpected guest, but smiled warmly.

"Clara, this is Elizabeth Southern."

"Mrs. Southern. Would you like some tea?"

"Yes. Yes, thank you, I would."

The long hall led back to a tall room with a sunken fireplace. The quaint and ultramodern blended in a pleasing harmony. The older woan re-entered witht tea, and set it on a dark carved table. Lili Black sat in a white modern chair facing Elizabeth Southern.

There was a quality about Lili Black which made Mrs. Southern at once secure and uneasy, a kind of strange, compelling magnetism. The lovely face would seem completely aloof as she asked pointed questions about the week past, until some word or phrase would suddenly animate it. Mrs. Southern tried her best to remember.

"When he came home on Wednesday, I knew something was wrong. Daneco, Henry's firm, had been talking merger with World Transport Enterprises for about six months. He was offered a phenomenal price to sell a controlling interest. The company has been sluggish lately, and a merger seemed the best answer.

"Naturally, my husband wanted to do some checking on the outfit he would be dealing with. He asked his 'contacts' to find out more about World Transport. Henry and I always discuss business matters, but he was very secretive about thie matter.

"Thursday night, he told me the merger was off, that WTE was into something 'very big and very dirty'—those were his words—and Daneco would sink or swim without their help. He seemed very upset."

"Upset? In what way?"

"He drank heavily. He kept saying things, like 'those bastards, those lousy bastards.' There were several calls that evening. Henry went into his study and I heard him shouting over the phone. He came out livid. He said he was going to see someone—a Mr. Winston—the next morning, and have it out with him."

"And the next morning?"

"He left the house early, saying he might be late getting home, and then . . ." She began to cry again. Clara sat beside her on the couch and gave her a handkerchief. Lili Black started to ask a question, but was stopped by a look from her companion.

After Elizabeth Southern regained her composure, Lili Black spoke again. "I have only one more question, Mrs. Southern. Did your husband have any history of heart trouble?"

"That's the strangest part. Henry suffered a series of mild heart attacks about ten years ago. His doctor said he was overweight and suffering from hypertension. He said that if Henry didn't change his habits drastically, he'd kill himself. Henry took it as a warning. He exercised in moderation, we took vacations, I made sure he had a safe diet. Then, last summer when we were in the Bahamas, a doctor friend gave him a complete checkup.

"He told him the damage to the heart tissue was

healed, and Henry would never have to worry again. It was like a reprieve from a death sentence. That's why I know . . ." Her voice faltered.

"That he was murdered."

"Yes."

Lili Black leaned closer to Mrs. Southern. A quiet coldness crept into her voice.

"You understand, Mrs. Southern, that the police will not be able to help you with this."

Elizabeth Southern nodded, mutely.

"You must trust me. What you've told me is very useful. Rest assured that your husband's death will receive justice."

For just a moment, Mrs. Southern caught a wild, intense gleam in Lili Black's eyes before she rose, smiling warmly, and said, "Well, thank you, Mrs. Southern. I hope our talk has been of some help to you. We must get together again soon, perhaps for lunch."

"Yes. I—I don't know how to thank you."

"That's quite all right. No thanks are necessary. Good night, Mrs. Southern."

"Good night."

* * *

Nightshade worked late into the night. In the laboratory of the clinic, she subjected the bloodstained blouse to rigorous chemical analysis. At last, just before dawn, she isolated the agent of Southern's death.

She recognized it as an extremely costly, little-known compound used exclusively by government intelligence agents to simulate heart attack in assassinations. Her hands clenched involuntarily when she realized the implications of her discovery.

The hunter's instinct had again led Nightshade to her prey. Once more, someone had stood in his way and was quickly and efficiently snuffed out. One more victim was dead. World Transport Enterprises was the key. In the heart of that vast conglomerate was the one she sought.

4

"World Transport, may I help you?" The phone was answered by a silver-haired woman in blue.

"Good morning, this is Tempo Temporary Service. You have a Miss Margo Jansen working with you?"

"That's right."

"Miss Jansen just called to notify us she will be unable to complete her four-week period. We are sending another girl this morning. Her name is Alison Clarke. She has the typing and stenographic skills you requested."

"Thank you." The executive secretary, Janet Hall, set down the receiver, making a mental note to tell her employer about the new girl.

A moment later, the doors of the express elevator opened. A tall man with a bony face stepped out. He was dressed well, in a tailored brown suit, with a brown shirt and cream tie. He held his hat in his large hands. He wore gloves.

"Mr. Winston?" His voice was deep, his hands moved nervously, and his words were carefully pronounced. There was a restrained violence about him that the woman behind the desk found unnerving.

"Who shall I say wishes to see him?"

A smile broke across his face which was more disconcerting than his somber expression.

"Bones. Just tell him Bones is here." She touched the intercom button on her phone.

"Mr. Winston, a Mr.—Bones to see you." There was a pause. "He says to go right in."

* * *

"What the hell do you mean by coming here!" Edward Winston's hands locked into the lapels of Bones's jacket. He threw Bones onto a black leather couch several feet away, and struck him across the face with the back of his hand in two brief strokes. A savage expression etched deep lines into his cheeks.

Bones cringed in shock and astonishment. Catching the reflection of Bones's fear, Winston collected himself, walked to the large glass window which spanned the wall of the office, straightened his tie, then re-emerged with deliberate calm.

Edward Winston was a regular-featured, almost bland businessman in his late forties. He worn a dark blue suit of conservative cut, a white shirt with a pale-blue design, and a striped silk tie.

At their last meeting, Bones sized Winston up as a creampuff, a weakling. Now, he realized he had made a mistake—maybe a fatal one. The nondescript exterior masked a cruel and volatile personality.

Winston spoke again, more calmly.

"I had hoped I was wrong about you, Bones, but I'm

afraid you've disappointed me. First, the theatrical death of Southern, virtually at my feet—and now, coming here in direct defiance of my orders, instead of waiting until the agreed meeting time." He seemed to be enjoying Bones's agitation.

"What did you hope to gain by coming here? Did you expect to get your money sooner? Were you planning to squeeze me for more?

"As it happens, Bones, I've already decided what to do about you. Your stupidity forced my hand." He crossed to his desk, then took an envelope from it.

"This contains a one-way ticket to Miami. There will be a reservation on the next flight in your name. When you arrive, you're to contact a man named Hunter. There's a little project in the works that you would be just perfect for. Not without risks, Bones, but not without its compensations—provided you come through in one piece. We wouldn't want to waste a man of your talents, would we?"

Winston's voice was calm, but Bones was horrified.

"Mr. Winston, I—I never . . ."

Winston cut him short. "Your plane is waiting. You wouldn't want to miss it."

Bones was halfway out the door when he heard Winston's final words: "And Bones, I don't expect to see your face, ever again."

Bones waited impatiently for the elevator. The doors opened, and he elbowed past a young, blonde woman who was getting out. As the doors slid shut, he noticed that she had turned to look at him.

The young woman paused, nodding slowly to herself, then turned, smiling brightly, to the woman behind the desk.

"Mrs. Hall? I'm Alison Clarke, from Tempo. I was assigned to work here for the next two weeks. The agency should have called you."

As the older woman took the form, she was startled by

the coldness of the girl's touch. She looked more closely at her. She looked efficient, not like the last two who had more charm than brains—still, she was pretty, and Mr. Winston liked them pretty.

"How's your steno?"

"I can do about a hundred."

"Good. You'll be busy today. There's always a lot of correspondence after the weekend."

Janet Hall showed her to a desk near the door to Winston's office and began to brief her on office procedure. Alison Clarke listened intently.

"Well, I think that's about it. Wm do you like to go to lunch?"

"About one or one-thirty. I like a late lunch."

"I usually go at noon. That should work out fine."

* * *

Winston glanced up from his desk as the new girl entered. His suite of offices was furnished in impeccable taste with modern furniture. His desk was massive, of dark wood, and virtually bare. An immense picture window commanded a dizzying view of the city.

He noted with appreciation her looks, figure, dress and tasteful use of makeup, then returned his thoughts to work.

"Miss Clarke, I have at least a dozen letters to get out by the end of the day. I hope I won't have to repeat myself."

"Oh no, sir."

"All right, then, memo: World Transport, District Chief, Sector Seven Marketing—George, semicolon—I find myself in an untenable position trying to defend the decline in the quality of our—services to the Midwestern Division, period. I can think of several people who will want an accounting very soon, and there's no time—no, strike that, very soon, period. If you can't come up with some—reasonable excuse by the end of the month, things could get very ugly. . . ."

* * *

Alison Clarke learned a great deal about World Transport that morning. As its name implied, it was active in both domestic shipping, and import and export. But it was also involved in petroleum research, international development, instrumentation, armaments, and long-range information research and planning. It had recently been awarded a government contract for chemical and biological research. In short, World Transport was typical of a late-twentieth century diversified multinational bureaucracy.

They were interrupted just before noon by the buzz of the intercom. Winston stabbed at the button.

"Yes?"

"Mr. Winston, I'm going to lunch now."

"Thank you, Mrs. Hall. Now, where were we?"

" '. . . long overdue, period'."

"Right. We cannot proceed without a complete accounting of the losses incurred during nationalization. Yours, etc. Next communication mark 'Confidential'. We're going to need a little background on this one." His hand hit the intercom.

Alison Clarke spoke quietly. "Mrs. Hall is at lunch, sir."

"Damn. Look, there's a key in her middle drawer. Use it to open the file room, and get me the file labeled USAF-6, second or third drawer."

"Yes, sir." Alison rose, returned to the outer office, and took a small key with a red tag from the desk. Winston did not look up as she crossed through his office to the file room beyond. She unlocked the door, and began to look through the drawers. A few minutes later, she heard Winston's voice.

"Miss Clarke, what's taking so long?"

"I'm sorry, Mr. Winston, I—I can't seem to find it."

He pushed back his chair, rose briskly. As he entered the file room, his eyes fixed on the open drawer. He strode forward and slammed it shut.

"I'll say this only once, so listen carefully. Don't *ever* go near that cabinet again!"

He turned to another chair and pulled out a file.

"Now let's get back to work. We've wasted enough time already!"

* * *

The following morning, as Alison Clarke was laying down her bag, Winston looked out the door of his office.

"Miss Clarke. Place a person-to-person call to a Mr. Carl Ramirez at this number—Santiago, Chile. I'll take it in my office."

"Right away, Mr. Winston."

She punched the number and waited for a response. Finally there was an answer.

"Carl Ramirez."

"I have a call from Edward Winston, World Transport."

"Go ahead." Winston picked up the line.

"Mr. Ramirez."

"Señor Winston? I was expecting your call. You are prepared to go ahead, then?"

"As soon as possible. How soon can you present the program to my men?"

"I can be in New York in forty-eight hours."

"Then I will expect you in time for an afternoon meeting, at 2:00 on Friday."

"I will be in your office first thing in the morning."

"Good. And one more thing—alert your organization. Things should move very quickly after this."

"As you wish."

After Winston ended the call, Alison lowered her receiver gently onto its cradle. A few moments later Winston emerged with a sheet of paper.

"When Mrs. Hall arrives, I want you to begin calling or cabling the people on this list. The message is brief. There will be a top-level urgent meeting, on my orders, in the executive board room at two o'clock, day after tomorrow. Make sure that every International District Vice President attends—and *no* excuses!"

"Yes, Mr. Winston."

* * *

That afternoon, when Janet Hall left for lunch, and Edward Winston was at a business conference, Alison was left alone in the office.

Reaching into Mrs. Hall's desk, she withdrew the red-tagged key, crossed through Winston's office and unlocked the file room door. She walked directly to one of the cabinets, opened it, and began a thorough and methodical search of the files. A photograph in a file labeled GANT, BENJAMIN 'BONES' caught her attention. It was the man she had seen on her first day. There was little information, except a note from Winston: *"Take out HMS, see TI file."* She continued through the files.

She was also drawn to the name RAMIREZ, CARL E. Withdrawing the file, she found it more informative. She began to look slowly through it. There was a complete and meticulous dossier on the man.

Ramirez was, it seemed, a "soldier of fortune," a professional insurgent and mercenary. Born of a German-American mother and an Argentine father, Ramirez spent the earlier part of his life in Switzerland, and the latter part in South America. A free-lance intelligence operative, he was also an accomplished smuggler, both of narcotics and guns; and a CIA-trained commando as well. A brief memo in Winston's hand referred again to a "TI file."

At last she came upon a thick folder, hand lettered in the broad felt-tip strokes of Edward Winston:

TERROR, INC.

She nodded to herself, opened it, and began to examine it in detail. The first words to catch her eye were "Terror Inc." It came as a shock when Alison checked her watch and realized she had been in the file room over an hour. Quickly, she replaced the folder, locked the door and was crossing back through Winston's office when his door opened.

Winston was surprised to see the new girl in his office. Before he could speak, she turned from his desk, holding out a sheet of paper and flashing a bright smile.

"I worked through lunch, Mr. Winston. Here's the list of cables. They've all been sent."

As he glanced over the list, she slipped silently out the door.

Late that afternoon, the first of the World Transport executives began arriving. Alison Clarke found herself involved in endless preparations for their travel and accommodations. From the red carpet treatment the airlines and hotels were giving them, it was clear that each was a very important man in his own right.

The following day was occupied in the preparation of information packets to be distributed at the Friday afternoon meeting. Edward Winston was in and out all day. A brusque tension was noticeable in his manner, and his instructions were terse and exacting. It was apparent that something extremely important was about to take place.

5

Friday morning, Alison glanced up to see a man looking intently down at her. He was not tall, perhaps five feet eight. His dark wavy hair gleamed with oil. He wore a tan linen shirt with short sleeves and military pockets. The mat of dark hair on his chest showed a touch of gray. His coloring was naturally light, but darkened to a leathery tan by sun and wind. His face was mobile and spare, the muscles articulate. His eyes were dark and predatory. For a moment, she returned his stare, then, looking down, spoke.

"Yes, sir. May I help you?"

"I am Carl Ramirez."

"Is Mr. Winston expecting you?"

"Yes."

"One moment, please."

Alison Clarke picked up the telephone, signalling Winston on the intercom.

"Yes?"

"Mr. Ramirez is here to see you, Mr. Winston."

"Tell him to cool his heels. I'll let him know when I'm free." The phone went dead.

"Mr. Ramirez, Mr. Winston is busy at the moment. Would you care to wait?" Ramirez flashed a fierce smile.

"I am at Mr. Winston's disposal." He sat in the reception area, and perused a copy of *Fortune* with barely restrained impatience. Mrs. Hall left to prepare the conference room. Ten minutes later, Alison was summoned into Winston's office. He turned to her.

"Tell Ramirez I have a few minutes." He turned his back.

"Yes, sir."

* * *

Winston did not rise when Ramirez entered. Ramirez laughed aloud, drew a Cuban cigar from his pocket, lit it, exhaled, and then posed a question: "Do you mind if I smoke?"

Winston barked a short laugh. "Shut the door, Ramirez. We don't have time for games."

"I quite agree, sir. Especially considering that I am charging you by the minute for the honor of my company—which brings us to the subject of money."

"Nothing to worry about if you do your part. Your advance is guaranteed. You and your people can draw against it as you wish. As soon as my men are briefed, you will have funds to go ahead with the pilot project."

"Ah, yes, the Carib operation. No second thoughts?"

"Only that there be no mishaps. If all goes well, we can begin to establish a more *permanent* arrangement."

"There will be no 'mishaps'."

"See that there are none. I will tolerate nothing less

46

than perfection."

"Very well, Señor Winston, but permit me to remind you of the terms of our agreement. *We* are the professionals. It must be done *our* way, or not at all . . ."

Hearing Mrs. Hall's footsteps returning down the corridor, Alison Clarke moved away from the office door.

* * *

By 1:30 P.M. the executive suite was alive with activity. Men whose bearing showed that they were accustomed to great power emerged from the express elevator singly and in pairs. Flanked by muscular young guards, they gave their names, glanced about, then headed down the corridor towards the conference area.

After the last of the executives had arrived, Alison Clarke reached into a bottom desk drawer. She took out a small stack of packets, and followed the executives to the conference area. As she approached the door to the conference room, two plainclothes guards stopped her.

"I'm sorry, miss, no one is permitted inside."

"But I have to deliver these packets."

One of the men took the packets.

"Don't worry, miss, we'll see that they're delivered." She hesitated, then smiled.

"Oh, thank you. Mr. Winston would be very angry at me if they weren't there in time for the meeting."

"Sure thing." Scanning the hall a final time, they turned and entered the conference suite. The lock turned with an audible click.

She stood a moment, considering the locked door. Her eyes narrowed in irritation. Then, as if in decision, she walked quickly to a nearby maintenance closet. She stepped inside and the door closed. The hall was empty.

In the darkened closet, Alison Clarke removed her blouse, skirt, and wig, revealing a close-fitting one-piece black garment and supple leather boots. With a shudder, the petite frame of the secretary unfolded into the lean and muscular body of Nightshade. Soft features became sharp and cold. Working in darkness, she stowed her clothing in her bag, dropped it to the floor, and turned her eyes to the closet ceiling.

The acoustical tile of World Transport's executive suite hung on a steel framework a foot below the ceiling. This false ceiling covered the entire suite of offices, providing a secret passage over walls and past locked doors Nightshade's mouth twitched in a half-smile thinking of the million-dollar security precautions so easily circumvented.

Stretching her arms, she lifted one of the panels and slid it aside. She grasped the supporting framework and swung her body up through the hole she had created. Resting on the framework, she slid the tile back, leaving it slightly askew to mark the closet. A checkerboard of steel stretched out for yards in all directions, broken occasionally by supports for fluorescent lights above translucent panels. She moved forward swiftly but carefully, never resting her full weight on the fragile acoustical panels.

From time to time she would lift one of the panels to check her position. As she neared the conference room, she peered down again. Two armed guards stood watch outside the door. Nightshade froze when the younger man suddenly looked up to scan the ceiling as if he noticed something. She lay motionless. After what seemed an eternity, he shifted his attention to his companion. Slowly, silently, she replaced the panel and inched the remaining feet forward. Again she looked down: she was directly over the center of the polished mahogany conference table.

The men who sat around it were, for the most part, middle-aged, with the confident weary eyes of men who ruled the world. Although the room was filled with luxurious appointments—their every need attended to

wordlessly—the executives seemed unaware of it all, as if this sort of opulence were taken for granted. A glance from Winston at the head of the table was all that was needed to bring them to attention. He rose.

"Thank you for taking the time to come here on such short notice. Our meeting today concerns a new direction for World Transport—a diversification, if you will, into a new area. Our guest is Carl Ramirez, who will present the program to you.

"Before he begins, however, I would like to stress three things. The first is that this is serious business, designed to benefit all of us. Second, Mr. Ramirez is a professional—the best in his business. I ask that you give him your undivided attention. The third is the need for absolute secrecy. For most of you, this will be your first and last direct contact with the program. It would be extremely unwise to discuss it outside this group." He paused to let his words sink in, then repeated, "Extremely unwise. Mr. Ramirez?"

Ramirez rose, surveying the gathering. A wide grin started on his face.

"Gentlemen, if I may have your attention. I know some of you are wondering about the purpose of this gathering. Mr. Winston here," he bowed slightly, "mentioned that it concerns 'diversification'. That, gentlemen, is in essence correct. However, this diversification is into an area in which most of you have little experience. It is for this reason that I was asked to join you today.

"You are, as I understand it, District Vice Presidents, assigned to particular geographic areas of the world. You will understand me, then, when I say that political considerations often affect your ability to freely exploit your market's potential. Local political events are often capricious and uncontrollable."

He swung his hand, leveling his finger at an older man across the table.

"Mr. Gonzalez. Several of your subsidiary operations

were nationalized by the Venezuelan government last month. You were powerless to stop them!"

His hand moved again.

"Mr. Grant, your electronics franchise has to yield thirty-six per cent of its profits to the Iraqi government."

And moved again.

"Mr. Carter, your East African plants have been the victims of assault six times in as many months! Gentlemen, forgive my bluntness, but it is time such events were not allowed to interfere with lawful commerce." His passionate oratory gave way to flat pragmatism.

"Gentlemen, the program we propose offers an alternative. I represent a group of professionals in the field of covert extralegal manipulation of world political events, through the use of strategically applied violence—in a word, *terrorism*." He regarded them keenly.

"Until now, we have worked only loosely as a team, but under my leadership we have begun to forge a highly effective international alliance. You will find in the packet before you a chart outlining the overall structure of the organization we propose. It is essentially this: One of our operatives will be assigned to work directly under each of you, in some minor administrative capacity. He will be your liaison to our agents in the field. If action needs to be taken, it can be relayed through the operative.

"The packets also contain brief reports of many of my organization's more recent successes. You will note that some of them are generally accepted to be the work of national liberation organizations. This method enables us to achieve our objectives and discredit our opposition simultaneously. We offer World Transport this unique consulting service on an exclusive basis. Gentlemen, the choice is yours."

Ramirez sat down and waited while the executives discussed the contents of the packets. When the discussion subsided, he rose again and asked for questions.

A lined older man in a gray suit spoke. "Marcotte, North Europe District. This is indeed a very impressive list, Mr. Ramirez. I had no idea all of these were your efforts. I for one would be glad to have your organization at my disposal. However, should one of your 'operatives' be captured, how do we avoid being—how shall I say it—*implicated?*"

"I understand your concern, Mr. Marcotte. A major advantage of our organizational structure is its built-in 'deniability factor'. The only people who will know the identity of the liaison will be the District Vice President, Mr. Winston and myself. Part of our agreement with World Transport is that each such operative is expendable, and will assume complete unilateral responsibility . . . should problems arise. A similar system has been used by Mr. Winston in his domestic operation quite successfully for the past few years.

"I must add . . . although my men are implicitly loyal, and I do not anticipate any difficulties, I have assured Mr. Winston that in the event an operative fails to meet this obligation, I will personally remedy the situation—immediately. Are there other questions?"

A clerkish man in his mid-thirties raised a hand. "May I ask Mr. Ramirez to outline his long-range plans for the program?"

"Certainly. Conditional upon approval, you should be seeing the results of our first pilot program. Mr. Winston requested that I say little more about it at this time. Should it prove successful, we can begin our program to aid World Transport companies in expanding operations into 'marginal areas' outside present markets. As a long-range goal we anticipate substantially increasing the size of your present territory by the support of favorable factions and the elimination of opposition forces who could limit free enterprise."

Ramirez looked around him. "Are there further questions? If not, then I would like to reiterate briefly why I believe this program will become necessary for any corporation of your scope. World Transport is a multinational organization, and although competition between Districts is encouraged, the highest goal is the good of the corporation as a whole. The day when the domestic squabbles of any country, even the United States, can be allowed to interfere with the demands of the free marketplace, is ending. The future is in our hands, gentlemen. We must manage that future deliberately, or our power to manage it will be taken from us!" Ramirez bowed curtly, and took his seat.

The executives had listened to the mercenary intently. When he concluded, there was a general murmur of approval. Winston nodded to Ramirez, then rose to his feet.

"I would like to thank Mr. Ramirez on behalf of the group for his excellent presentation. If there are no objections, I move we give the proposal a vote of confidence. Those of you who are in accord with adopting the program immediately, signify by saying 'aye'—those opposed, 'no'."

There were no dissenting voices.

* * *

Nightshade nodded grimly from her place of concealment, her most extreme conjectures totally confirmed. This new information would involve her more deeply than ever in this fledgling "Terror, Inc.," but it was essential that she learn more. Somewhere behind these men, perhaps in this very room, was her prey—the man for whom she had prepared herself for the past decade.

* * *

After a few minutes of conversation, the meeting started to break up. As the District Vice Presidents were leaving the room, they paused to shake Ramirez's hand, saying they were glad to have him "on the team." A short time later, only Winston and Ramirez were left.

"Well done, Ramirez. They seem sold on the program. The sooner you can round up your people, the better."

"I can arrange for the Miami meeting to take place within a week. I am afraid some of my associates are unable to travel as freely as your colleagues. Perhaps you could use your influence in a few cases."

"You have the full weight of World Transport behind you, Ramirez. Whatever you need, get it. Hunter will provide the 'specialists' you requested for 'Carib.' I've just assigned one of my domestic operatives to him. I think he's the ideal man—a bit headstrong, but good. And remember, I meant what I said earlier: My team will be watching 'Carib' with keen critical interest."

* * *

Watching the two men shaking hands and preparing to leave, Nightshade knew it was time to end her vigil. She moved swiftly back to the closet, lowered herself down the repositioned panel. She assumed again the guise of Alison Clarke and slipped out the closet door. As it closed behind her, Winston and Ramirez emerged from the suite. She froze, waiting to see if they would challenge her presence in the restricted area.

But neither of the men gave her a second glance: She was as much a part of the landscape to them as the walls and the wastebaskets. It was ironic that two professionals, who achieved their position due to a talent for observation and self-preservation, not even noticing that they were being observed—simply because she was the obvious and ever-present secretary. Such blindness would prove their downfall.

6

That evening, sitting at home, staring into the flames, Nightshade's thoughts were interrupted by a clear voice. "What is it, dear? You've been brooding about something for hours."

Nightshade turned, almost smiling, and faced the older woman. "I was not aware you could read my mind, Clara."

"I know you well. What have you discovered?"

Slowly at first, Nightshade recounted what she learned about World Transport's unholy alliance with terrorists and mercenaries.

"Don't you see, Clara? With an army like this, he could gain a stranglehold on half the world! Somehow I must find him. Stop him!"

"Why? For the sake of the thousands of innocent lives

that would be damaged? Or for yourself—for the banishment of that old spectre?"

Nightshade shut her eyes, shutting out her friend's words. "I don't know what you're talking about."

"Let's call it by its proper name—*Vengeance*. Do you think you have any secrets from me? I made you what you are, shaped your mutilated flesh into what it is today. I gave you skills to make of yourself whatever you chose. Do you believe in all that time I had no idea what motivated you, what drove you to perfect yourself, turn your body and mind into the instruments they are now?"

Clara drew a deep breath, and continued more softly, "I had such hopes for you. I prayed that you would give this up, that you would turn your talents to some constructive human use. Yet, you persist. My dear child, can't you see that if you continue this quest of yours, you will become no better than him?"

Nightshade sank back into her chair and stared into the flames. When she answered, it was in a whisper.

"I have no choice. *He* made me what I am, just as much as you did. You repaired the outside, and, perhaps, the inside as well. But *he* killed my past, everything I was and could have been. Until he has atoned for that, I cannot call my life my own."

Nightshade halted, seeing at last the pain in her friend's face. "I love you, Clara, you know that. I owe you everything. But I can't give this up now. I *may* not give it up. Please, try to understand."

The white-haired woman moved close to Nightshade, and took her icy hands. There were tears in her eyes.

"I know I can't stop you, child. I only hope—he doesn't kill you again." Clara sighed, forced a smile. "So where does this lead now?"

Grimly, Nightshade replied, "Miami."

7

Aaron Meyer was delighted at the prospect of presenting Doctor Black to the exclusive audience of the Albemarle Hotel. The style and grace of the lady magician was a drawing card which would bring the northern weekenders to his hotel even in the heat of summer. Lately he had been forced to give up his exclusive Jewish clientele and take wealthy Cuban and Puerto Rican customers. Aaron Meyer did not believe in discrimination—he was kicked out of too many hotels in his youth to feel that way. It was, he told himself, a matter of style, a touch of *class* which he did not find in his Latin customers.

This should be a very good weekend for him—two shows and a press party. The publicity from this could keep him for a year. He hummed to himself while he sorted the display cards for the lobby. The striking face and figure of the magician was superimposed over tall thin letters spelling out DOCTOR BLACK, and the dates. Yes indeed, this should be a *very* good weekend.

* * *

It was Clara's idea to arrive for a brief television interview at the airport. The magician stepped from the gate in a loose white pantsuit, a broad-brimmed straw hat, and large oval sunglasses. She moved with an almost exaggerated glamour. As the camera crew set up, she fixed a mysterious smile on her face, and advanced to shake hands with the local press.

A woman in orange, with a slight southern accent, turned to the camera, microphone in hand.

"We're about to witness the arrival of Doctor Black, the marvelous magician who has fascinated us so much lately with the art of illusion. Tell me, Doctor Black, do you believe in magic? I mean with a capital 'M'?"

Doctor Black smiled and plucked a rose from the interviewer's sleeve, and presented it to her, saying, "Do you?"

A murmur of delight and approval rose from the gathering. The lady thanked the magician and returned to her question.

"Seriously—I'm sure our viewers would like to know what a stage magician feels about all this occult activity, horoscopes, witchcraft and all that."

Doctor Black smiled, a sparkle alive in her eyes.

"Well," she said, "anything's possible, isn't it?" With

that, she vanished in a puff of smoke.

The commentator was stunned for a moment, her astonishment getting the better of her professional sense. Then she turned to the camera and said, "This is Arlene Davis, for Action News."

* * *

The press party was going strong, with only one minor drawback. The star attraction had not yet arrived. At one end of the room was a buffet which Aaron Meyer catered himself. The other held only a circular pedestal, draped in black velvet. Suddenly a blinding light appeared above the platform, surrounded in a swirling cloud of smoke. The mist changed from white to rose to gray, and back to white. It parted, and Doctor Black stepped down.

She was dressed in a black velvet version of a traditional magician's costume, with a white turtleneck. A slim wand of silver rested in one hand. The photographers were caught unaware, but were now snapping picture after picture. She was immediately surrounded by a crowd of excited press who had heard of her fabulous stunt at the airport just moments ago from one of the newspaper stringers. She would say nothing, save that she was tired from her trip and wanted a few minutes to freshen up. She stepped into a private salon prepared for her, and closed the door.

Minutes passed as she stared at the window in her dressing room, waiting. Finally there was a tap on the glass. She opened the window to admit another Doctor Black in white. Rapidly the newcomer changed into an identical costume. At the same time, the other removed a dark wig to reveal white hair. Her eyes twinkled at the deception.

"I haven't had so much fun in years. It was just like the old days . . ." As she spoke, Clara dressed herself in a loose tweed suit. Just ten minutes from the time she entered the room, Doctor Black emerged, accompanied by her elder companion.

"And now, ladies and gentlemen . . ." She waved her sterling wand, "Champagne!" A bottle of excellent domestic champagne appeared in her hand, wrapped in a cloth.

"Glasses, please." As a queue of interested press presented their glasses, she asked each in turn what they would prefer—white, pink, or sparkling burgundy. To each she poured the proper shade.

One older man demurred and said, "Nothing alcoholic for me, I'm afraid."

The magician took his glass and filled it with ginger ale! By the time the fifteenth glass had been filled, a buzz of amazement spread through her onlookers.

Finally, a brash young reporter challenged her, stating, "I would prefer Cold Duck."

She snapped a cool glare at him. Then she smiled again, and reached into his coat. She pulled out a rubber toy duck, and handed it to him.

"For your bath! Next, please!"

The room resounded with laughter, and the young man tried to make himself as invisible as an ordinary mortal could. Doctor Black performed several more stunts, finishing with roses for the ladies, and cigars for the gentlemen. Then she perched on top of her velvet pedestal to field questions.

From the back of the room:

"Doctor Black, how do you manage your incredible illusions?"

"Very carefully. Next?"

"Where did you learn the art of magic?"

"In Hamburg, 1936."

A man in front:

"But you couldn't have been more than two years old!"

"Perhaps you're right."

A woman to the left:

"To what do you attribute your fantastic popularity, Doctor Black?"

"The sense of wonder."

At precisely five o'clock, the magician excused herself to prepare for her performance. One reporter buttonholed her companion at the door.

"Tell me the truth. Did she really disappear at the airport?"

Clara leaned close and whispered conspiratorially, "No. She's still there. It *is* all done with mirrors, you know." Smiling sweetly, the older woman followed Doctor Black through the door.

The magician stood by the window, her hands behind her back.

"Clara, I sometimes wonder if all this is necessary."

"Of course it is. Nothing arouses more unhealthy interest than a secretive celebrity. It's all part of the role you have chosen to play. You must learn to live with it, dear."

"You're right as always, Clara. What would I ever do without you?"

"It's getting late—we'd better go set the stage."

·8

Nothing Aaron Meyer had ever seen compared with the reception that Miami afforded Doctor Black. Even after limiting the premiere customers to season regulars, the hall was packed, and there was standing in the rear! It was incredible. Meyer had booked a couple of magicians back in the lean days, but nothing he could recall matched the drawing power of this act. A Streisand, a Goulet maybe even a Vikki Carr drew these crowds, but a *magician*? Never.

Yet, here they were: furs dripping over the backs of seats, diamonds and paste sparkling in the house lights, a pitch of excitement unparalleled in his memory. Slipping away from the door, he stationed himself in the first row center seat, and waited for the curtain. Everything was planned in secret—he had no idea what to expect. And this was a tough crowd. But she was a pro, this one, and something was in the air. Meyer leaned back to watch.

From nowhere, music sounded, somewhat classical, somewhat exotic, as the curtains parted. The stage was bare. The audience waited.

Suddenly there was a crash like a gong or cymbal. There was a frightening flash of light and a scent of ozone, and Doctor Black appeared as if deposited by a thunderbolt. She bowed to the applause, then waved her hand, and it stopped. White hands gesticulated in the air and plucked from nothingness a large mottled-orange egg.

"You have heard the legend of the Phoenix—the bird that lays its egg in flames, and is consumed, only to be born again . . ."

She handed the flame-colored egg to a waiting assistant. Gesturing with her left hand, she produced a crimson scarf. She snapped it into the air and it settled on the top of an unseen table before her. As the music became sinuous and faintly eastern, her hands continued to conjure. In an instant she had placed on the cloth a gleaming brazier alive with flames leaping several feet in the air.

Slowly, she began to turn back the sleeves of her dark coat, and the white lace blouse beneath. Retrieving the egg from her assistant, and holding it in the palm of her hand, she thrust her arm into the flames. The audience gasped as if sensing the pain. The magician did not flinch.

There was a pause, then the flames vanished. In their place was a flame-colored bird of paradise resting on the magician's wrist. As the applause began, Doctor Black bowed deeply, her arm extended. Then, floating the crimson scarf over the bird, she vanished it from sight. The applause continued, louder now, and the magician smiled briefly.

As the sound began to die, she removed her dark coat. She motioned to the wings. Two assistants in black wheeled onstage a great shining metal fan, mounted on a high steel rack.

"Ladies and gentlemen, you see a heavy-duty industrial fan, whose blades have been especially sharpened for this presentation. Observe."

She activated the fan. With a clatter, the three blades began to spin. The clatter became a whine and then a roar, as the blades became invisible. An assistant handed Doctor Black a length of wood which she tossed into the whirling heart of the fan. A spray of fine wood chips showered from the fan, with no appreciable change in its momentum.

Doctor Black spoke again in a clear raised voice.

"You will agree, ladies and gentlemen, that it would be unwise to try to pass anything through the blades of the fan while it is operating."

The magician swiveled the fan parallel to the floor, causing the curtains to billow, and her hair to fly about.

"Gentlemen, if you please."

The assistants began to bind her hands behind her back, and then her ankles. A stout cable dropped down from center stage, and was attached to her by a clip.

"I will be drawn up by this cable. At the signal, the cable supporting me will release—dropping me through the blades of the fan. If I may have absolute silence, please."

The cable grew taut, and the magician was lifted off the stage. The ascent was slow, and she swung gently in the powerful breeze of the fan. Finally she stopped. Her face became grave. She hung motionless.

A cymbal crashed. The magician plummeted into the murderous blades.

Seconds later, she was crouched below the fans, unhurt. Then she sprang forward into the spotlight, the ropes still hanging from her wrists and ankles, severed, as if by a sharp knife. She bowed low as the audience applauded. The assistants removed the fan from the stage.

* * *

All eyes were on the magician as she gracefully accomplished the levitation of a young lady from the audience. When the volunteer was again on her feet, she seemed dazed, as if unable to remember what had happened. The audience gave the bewildered girl a warm round of applause.

Doctor Black followed the illusion with a series of dazzling hand productions, filling the air with silks, coins, cards and colored balls. The dignified audience had become a cheering crowd.

Finally Doctor Black gestured for silence.

"For my final illusion, I am presenting for the first time what I call the Vanishing Curtain."

She gestured offstage and a steel cart was wheeled in. On the top of the cart was a great ceramic jar of pale blue, about three feet in diameter. The cart was stationed at the extreme right of the stage. On the extreme left was placed a small trampoline. Doctor Black signalled, and a metal frame was stretched across the stage, perpendicular to the back curtain. The magician pulled a deep blue cloth from the bottom of the cart, and shook it out.

"This curtain," she said, "was manufactured by an old and illustrious firm in Old Delhi, India. Its purpose is to make things disappear. For example . . ." She threw the sheet over the cart. It dropped flat to the surface as if the jar were not there. She then whisked it away . . . the jar had returned.

She rapped the globe of ceramic with her wand. It rang faintly.

"This evening, *I* am going to vanish. Gentlemen?"

The assistants took the cloth from her and stretched it across the frame, attaching it with clips. The magician tapped the cloth with her hand and it vibrated like a drumhead.

"I will now attempt to dive through the Vanishing Curtain. If all goes well, I should vanish. If there are any problems . . ." The exaggerated gravity of her manner was almost a parody of her previous patter—as if some deadly peril awaited one who misused the cloth.

Mounting to the trampoline, she leapt gracefully into the air, higher each time. Then, with the full momentum of her leap, she dove forward, toward the Vanishing Curtain.

A thousand watchers saw her hit the cloth. It did not tear or part—she did not rebound. She had vanished.

The audience was stunned. For a time there was silence as the stage again stood bare. Aaron Meyer began to squirm, wondering if she might have pulled the same trick she had at the airport.

Then a woman cried, "It's moving!"

She was right. The blue-white jar on the cart had begun to tremble. It began a rocking motion, tipping further with each swing. As it neared the edge, it started to tip over—then fell.

A triumphant Doctor Black sprang from the shards, taking a deep bow as the curtains closed. Meyer was on his feet, pounding his palms together, before he knew it. This act had *class*. Swiftly he ran backstage to congratulate her on her performance.

"Beautiful! Just beautiful!"

The magician barely smiled. Slowly she extended her hand. Meyer found himself involuntarily on his knees, pressing his lips to the back of her hand. The commanding power of her eyes was hard to bear.

A voice from behind him broke her spell.

"Lili! There you are, dear. Come, we mustn't keep Mr.

Meyer. I'm sure he has things to do."

The magician's face relaxed, and she forced a lovely smile.

"Do get up, Mr. Meyer. You embarrass me."

She whirled away, leaving him stunned at her hypnotic effect on him. He watched as the tall woman and her companion disappeared down the narrow stairway to her dressing room, and shook his head. Then he shrugged . . . as long as it paid the bills, he had no business complaining.

In the dressing room, Lili Black turned to her companion.

"Well, how was I?"

The older woman regarded the younger.

"Better, much better. You've learned to relax on stage, or perhaps . . ."

"Perhaps what?"

"I think at times the old fears are still there, just buried very deep. Well, it does not matter. You are everything I hoped you would be. This was a cold audience, and you were mistress of them all."

As the magician stripped off the dark costume, the light illuminated faint traceries of scars on her upper arms and thighs. She dressed consciously, pulling on a loose tan suit, belted with a sash. She covered her piercing gaze with a pair of large tinted glasses, then cocked her head, smiling at the effect in the mirror.

"Well, let's be off. Our public waits."

9

The Top of the Town is a swank supper club on the top floor of the Albemarle. At Clara's insistence, Lili Black had accepted a dinner invitation from Wade Beaumont, the influential editor-publisher of *Southways*. Beaumont was preceded by a reputation as a playboy, sportsman and canny businessman. The meeting was to plan a feature for the newspaper supplement on magic in general and Doctor Black in particular.

The two women arrived in the cocktail lounge across from the elevator, and a tall muscular man with crinkling blond hair rose from the bar to greet them. He looked deeply tanned, but the magician noticed a paleness about his wrists and neck, which led her to believe the tan had come from a bottle.

He smiled a broad, tooth-filled grin, and extended his hand. "Doctor Black! I've been looking forward to meeting you." As his hand gripped hers, he flinched slightly. "Our table is waiting."

Doctor Black introduced Clara to Beaumont. He was cordial as he led them to a table in an isolated section. Through the glass windows of the restaurant, they could see Miami Beach gleaming below them.

"Now then," began Beaumont, "tell me a little about yourself, uh—Miss, er . . ."

"Doctor Black."

"Right. Doctor Black Well, tell me a little about yourself."

"What would you like to know?"

"Oh, just the juicy details—where you were born, when, height, weight, color of eyes, favorite perfume—you know, something to interest the ladies and gents who read my rag." There was an icy silence.

Finally Clara spoke. "Doctor Black never speaks of her past."

"Uh-huh. Okay, right. Well, then—tell me, how did you get into show business, Doc?"

"Through a love of the craft, and a need for money."

"Right. What I need is something I can *print*, you know, like . . . 'dreamed of being a magician as a little girl,' that sort of thing."

"Please don't let me stop you from writing what you think will interest your readers."

"Yeah. I just need a little background, you know, something to work with."

"Background? But I have no *background*."

"Well, what did you do before you became a presti-whatchamacallit?"

"I was a professor at Heidelberg."

"You're kidding, right? No, I guess not. Oh! I get it. The *enigma* bit. Like: 'who is this mysterious Doctor Black who's taking the country by storm . . .' Is that it? You know, I like it. It's a dynamite angle. The kids will eat it up. I like your style, Doc. We should see some more of each other while you're in town. See the sights, get to know each other better . . ."

"Why?"

For a moment Beaumont stared at her.

"Oh, just a thought. You know, thought you might like some company while you're in town. Just a thought. Say! How did you do that disappearing act at the airport? That really had them gaping."

The magician raised one eyebrow, almost amused.

"Shall we tell him, Clara?"

"I think not, dear. If the secret should get out, no one in America would be safe." Except for the twinkle in the older woman's eyes, one would have taken the comment as a statement of fact.

There was another flat silence.

"Well," said the man at last, "shall we order dinner?"

At that, the magician snapped her fingers, and drew the waiter. Almost in a trance, he asked what she would be having. She ordered a twelve-ounce steak, raw, half a head of lettuce with oil and vinegar, and black coffee.

"The gentleman will be having chicken *cordon bleu*, tossed salad with Roquefort dressing, and—oh, yes—a whiskey sour, straight up."

Beaumont was dumbfounded.

"Now, how in hell did you know that?"

"By magic, of course. Who do you think you're dealing with, a juggler?"

Beaumont looked sheepishly at the waiter.

"What the lady said—but that sour is on the rocks. Do you mind if I smoke?"

Hands trembling slightly, he pulled a cigar from his jacket. The magician snapped her fingers and produced a flame.

"Uh—thanks."

"Not at all."

The dinner proceded without further incident until dessert. Wade Beaumont had never known a woman like

Lili Black before. She was confident, independent and brash, and his questions had produced not one clear fact by the end of the meal. There wasn't a woman who hadn't eventually succumbed to his charm, his good looks, or his money, so he decided to redouble his efforts.

"You know, Doc, there's something about you I like. You're a different breed of cat, if you know what I mean. Why people like you and me have to deal with the day to day business the rest of these bozos do, is beyond me. Why, if we stick together, I can show you a side of this town you've never . . ." Suddenly she swung round and stared at him, a strange expression on her face. He froze, unable to say another word.

"I must apologize, Mr. Beaumont, I wasn't listening. I was—distracted."

During dinner, Nightshade noticed a man sitting alone, watching the entrance from behind a newspaper. In two hours he smoked nine cigarettes and consumed four cups of coffee, but had not ordered dinner. As she watched, he put down the paper and rose as another man entered. When she recognized the man who arrived, she turned quickly back to Beaumont.

"You must excuse me."

Before he could stop her, Nightshade was out of her seat, laying a twenty on the table. She hesitated a moment, giving the two men time to leave, then slipped after them out into the night. Beaumont stared after her, shaking his head.

"I don't understand it."

"That's strange," said Clara, "*I* understand perfectly."

She stood up and put on her gloves. "Do forgive this little interruption. I'm sure we'll be back in touch soon. Good night, Mr. Beaumont."

"Good night." Beaumont turned to a corner of the room. "Waiter! Another whiskey sour—*straight up!*"

10

Harold Hunter was relieved when the man he was waiting for finally arrived. He was afraid he was beginning to appear conspicuous. His guest, a professional executioner named Benjamin "Bones" Gant, arrived over an hour late. As soon as the formalities were out of the way, Hunter suggested that they adjourn to one of his favorite watering holes. Reluctantly, Bones agreed. Hunter paid the bill, and they rose to go. Out of habit, Hunter checked to see if he was being followed. He saw no one.

The sultry evening air of Miami Beach was touched with a tang of salt and oil. The rows of tall, monolithic hotels were islands of light, and the streams of traffic stroboscopically wound their way between them. Hunter, moving fast, was crossing the street, dodging cars with Bones following behind, bemused and a little annoyed.

To Hunter it was a tactic to throw Bones off balance until they reached the bar.

It lay hidden between a gift shop and a travel agency, in the basement floor of an older hotel. The sea smells mingled with the olive oil and salted nuts of the bar's interior, and the traffic noise was drowned out by the music of Tito Puente on the tinny juke box.

Most of the customers were Latin. Most of them were also men. One tall woman sat alone in a booth, a double scotch in front of her, half-drained, and an ashtray of lipstick-stained cigarette butts beside her, glancing in irritation at her watch. Something about her held Bones for a moment, then it passed, and he followed Hunter toward a darkened nook at the end of the bar, near the men's room and a mechanical bowling machine.

There was little headroom and no legroom for Bones on the bench across from Hunter. Hunter ordered a scotch and soda in Cuban Spanish, while Bones tried to fit his frame into the booth.

Harold Hunter was a small man. His nose was an exaggerated slope ending in a ridiculous ball. His face had a rumpled look of injured nobility. He professed to be a writer, and enjoyed modest sales of a few dime novels about a debonnaire international spy named St. Clair.

His real profession, however, was as an *operative*—a man with sufficient intelligence to take an order and make it a reality, but with enough loyalty to his employer not to ask questions. He believed he was defending the Free World from a great amorphous force which he associated vaguely with Communists, homosexuals and demons. Anyone or anything which opposed those forces commanded his loyalty.

When Hunter learned that Bones was being assigned to his jurisdiction, he studied his dossier carefully. Bones's main assets seemed to be stamina, ruthlessness, and a steady hand—exactly the qualities such a man would need for the difficult but vital mission ahead. But men like Bones were brutal and volatile, and needed to be handled carefully and firmly.

Bones was also sizing up Hunter. He had been given his fee for the Southern contract on the flight to Miami, and had spent the last few days blowing it. When Hunter's call came, Bones was trying in vain to get something started with a classy lady who worked as a waitress in his hotel. He would have preferred to be back with her at the hotel now, even though he hadn't been able—after buying her drinks and doing a lot of fancy talking—to get as much as a seductive smile.

But Bones knew the Hunter assignment was his last chance to prove himself. If he blew this one, he was dead—literally.

Bones shifted awkwardly in the cramped seat. "What's this job you got for me?"

Hunter smiled. "What's your hurry, Bones? Have a drink! Take it *easy*!"

Bones started to press the point, then thought about the way Hunter pronounced the word "easy." There was enough venom there for Bones to order a double, drain it, and push the glass across the table.

Hunter moved Bones's glass back a few inches.

"Ever been to Miami, Bones?"

"I done some time here, yeah."

Bones moved an ashtray closer to Hunter. He lit a slim cigar, and tossed the match over the ashtray. It landed in front of Hunter. Hunter brushed it from the table.

"This is a pretty big assignment, Bones. One of vital importance to our free enterprise system, and perhaps the entire world."

Bones kept his teeth together. He worked with flag-wavers before, and their money was just as green as anybody else's. He made allowances.

"Now I don't expect *that* to move you as much as the hundred thousand," said Hunter, "but I wanted to make clear just what it is we're fighting for."

"Okay, I'll bite. Who's the mark? Some two-bit Commie dictator?"

Hunter's knuckles went white, but he betrayed no other sign of irritation.

"This is not the kind of business you discuss casually in public places." He drew a magazine from his coat, and placed it open before Bones. An old newspaper clipping had been stuck in it. "Your mission, Mr. Gant, concerns the individual circled in this photograph."

While Bones examined the clipping, Hunter noted his expression intently. Bones whistled low under his breath.

"I gather you recognize the man, Mr. Gant."

Bones nodded.

"Very well." Hunter took back the magazine. "In a moment I'm going to hand you an envelope. It contains a key to a bus locker in the downtown station where you will find the name of your contact, the necessary papers, and your retainer. The remainder of the money will be waiting for you on your safe return. The men you shall associate with are professionals. Trust them. I will be back in touch later."

He gave Bones a meaningful look.

"Remember, Bones, this isn't one of your cheap gangland hits. This is serious business. If you default on your agreement—you die."

With that, Hunter rose, tossing an envelope on the table with a melodramatic flourish.

Bones sat, staring at the envelope. Then, pulling a knife from his pocket, he slit it open.

He drained his coffee, pocketed the key, and crumpled the envelope into his pocket. He tossed a few coins on the table and walked out of the bar.

Bones flagged a cruising cab, got in, leaned back saying only, "Bus Station." The cabbie realized his fare meant business, and delivered him in record time. Bones paid the driver, entered the station, glanced behind him, and strolled to the designated locker. Inside he found a large brown packet and a small white envelope. He put the packet into his coat pocket and opened the white envelope. It contained only a cryptic note, two words in red ink: "*Ramirez/McCall*."

He slammed the locker door, and, striding to the information window, demanded, "McCall—which way?" A bored old man with dark leathery skin looked up from his *Herald* to answer, "Hotel McCall? Flagler, at Biscayne. Ask anyone."

Bones sauntered out the door, turned left, and soon came within sight of the hotel. He had that prickly feeling that he was being followed, and turned slightly, as if the wind made it hard to light his cigar. Looking out over the cupped flame of his match, he scanned the street. No one—probably nerves. This contract could get him killed.

The night clerk looked up when he walked in the door. The clerk was about sixty and wearing an immaculately pressed but frayed suit. He spoke up in a hoarse voice, "Yes, sir. May I help you?"

"Yeah," said Bones. "Name's Bones. Message for me from a Ramirez?"

"Just a moment, Señor." The clerk made an elaborate ritual of taking a pair of gold rimmed half-glasses out of his breast pocket, placing them on his nose, and examining several slips of paper in turn.

"Ah, yes. Here it is, Señor. Señor Ramirez is expecting you in suite 705. You may take either elevator." He looked up expectantly for a tip. He was disappointed.

An old woman in a slovenly operator's uniform was sitting inside the elevator, reading a *fotonovela*. Bones told her the suite number, and she slowly activated the car. When the doors opened, he stepped out, turned right, and was met by a man with a gun. His hand flew to his shoulder, but the man had already lowered his gun and pointed with it to a door. He motioned Bones inside.

* * *

Carl Ramirez had heard the elevator creak its way up to the floor, had heard the doors open, and sank back into a soft chair, half in shadow, to wait for his visitor. The chair opposite him, in full light was intended for Bones. Ramirez believed in the value of a psychological advantage when meeting a man for the first time. He wondered what sort of man this would be—Hunter's hired killer, a product of World Transport's millions.

The door swung open, and Bones entered first, then Ramirez' gunman. Ramirez barely restrained a curse.

"Mr. Gant?" Ramirez' voice was half questioning, hoping there had been a mistake.

"You Ramirez? Hunter told me to see you. Said you had a job for me."

"Mr. Gant," repeated Ramirez, "I am afraid there has been a mistake. A deadly mistake."

"Hey, I'm s'posed to see a guy named Ramirez. I asked you if you was him." Bones's hand inched to his shoulder. Ramirez waved him to the chair.

"Sit down, Bones. I am Carl Ramirez. Am I to understand that you are the man Hunter assigned to this operation?"

"You mean knocking off that island king-pin? Man, this ain't gonna be an easy one! I sure hope you have a good back-up crew. A guy could get killed!"

Ramirez closed his eyes and mumbled an *ave maria* under his breath. He looked again at the assassin.

"Bones, what makes you think that any back-up crew, even the best, can get *you* in and out of that island?"

Anger tightened Bones's face. "What the hell do you mean by that? This is *Bones Gant* you're talking to. I'm the best hit-man in this whole damn country. I can get in and out of anyplace you care to name. I can shake any tail you can put on me. I mean *any*! Nobody even sees me if I don't want them to. And one more thing. I *never* miss."

Ramirez' temper flared.

"Look here, you idiot! Didn't that jackass Hunter tell you? This island is *black*. Every man, every woman, every child. How are you going to move? You can't walk down a street in Port-au-Prince without being spotted! If you're white, you're a foreigner! And no foreigner gets within a mile of the *Président* without an armed guard." Ramirez' tone was biting. Bones flushed a deep red, and rose to his feet.

"It ain't my job to get myself close. *You* get me close! I pull the damn trigger. If you're good enough to work with Gant, you're good enough to get me in."

"*Mr. Gant*—" Ramirez controlled his fury—"I am afraid I cannot risk this mission, and the lives of my agents, on your ability. Hunter made a mistake. You may well be a fine assassin, but you are useless to this operation." Ramirez turned quickly and left the room, slamming the door behind him.

Bones looked around, still fuming. He spotted liquor bottles, and went over to pour himself a drink. Useless, was he? He tossed down the whiskey, poured another. This Ramirez character was crazy. What did he want—some *nigger* to make the hit? Bones snorted at the idea.

A door behind him opened and Bones turned, ready to tell Ramirez what he thought of him. His eyes widened at what he saw. Maybe his luck wasn't so bad after all. There, standing barefoot in the doorway, was the most beautiful woman Bones had even seen. She was wearing a white crepe jumpsuit with a plunging neckline. Her hair was long and richly dark, her eyes black.

The woman was startled to see Bones.

"Where—where is Carlos? I thought he was in here." She spoke in a musical Spanish accent. Bones decided to turn on the charm.

"Well, pretty girl, he ain't here just now, but I am. My name's Bones, Bones Gant. What's your name?" Bones was stalking toward the woman as he spoke. "Why don't you just come on over here, an' we can get acquainted."

The woman backed away, and Bones grinned. That was okay. Bones liked his girls a little frightened. His hand darted out and grabbed her wrist.

"You're hurting my arm!" she gasped.

"I asked you your name." Bones twisted the woman's wrist.

"Elena! My name is Elena! Please let go!" She struggled to release herself, but he grabbed hold of her hair and snapped her head back.

"Good girl. Now, Elena," Bones sneered into her face, jerking her arm up behind her, "give me a little kiss, Elena. C'mon, relax." Bones snickered at the shock in Elena's eyes. He held her tightly and pressed his mouth to her lips.

Elena struggled, beating at his head with her free hand. He released her mouth, and she screamed loudly, but only once. Bones's fingers gripped her throat and tightened, cutting off any further sound.

"You shouldn't yell like that, girlie. I didn't want to hurt you, but. . ." He let go of her arm and slapped her, then struck her again with the back of his hand.

* * *

On the window ledge outside, a black clothed form lay ready to spring into the room. Nightshade waited silently, hearing the argument, and did not intend to be seen. Bones's advances at the woman disgusted her, but when he attacked Elena, all instincts drove Nightshade to strike.

Just when Bones struck Elena the second time, the door burst open. Carl's face turned white at what he saw. He seized a gun from one of the guards who flanked him on both sides.

"Let go of my woman, fool!"

Bones confronted him, but did not release Elena.

Ramirez stepped forward, and repeated the order.

"Carlos, help me!" Elena sobbed.

Bones pushed the woman away, and reached for his own weapon. Before he could draw it, Ramirez fired, one shot, through the heart. Bones whimpered, then fell to the floor.

Elena rushed to Ramirez, clinging to him.

"Carl! He was going to—to. . .I tried to stop him and. . ." She began to weep, her shoulders heaving with sobs. Carl took her by the shoulders, led her into the bathroom. He splashed cold water on her, then thrust a towel in her face. Gradually her gasping subsided.

Ramirez disengaged himself and walked into the living room where he picked up the hotel phone and barked, "Room service? Three bags of ice, *por favor*. What? For a party. . .*Gracias*." He returned to the room. Elena stood by the window.

He called to a guard. "Take his feet. Let's get him into the bathtub. Not a word of this to anyone, do you understand?" The guard nodded.

Carl lifted the bloodied form by the armpits, dragging it slowly into the bathroom. The guard supported the feet. They tumbled it into the tub, and ran water over the body. The doorbell rang.

Carl strode to the door. The bellman delivered the ice, accepted the generous tip, and vanished without a word. Carl wheeled the cart into the bathroom and poured ice over Bones's corpse, then left the bathroom to its grisly occupant.

Back in the bedroom, Elena swayed and slumped to the floor. Entering, Carl swore softly, rushed forward and lifted her up into his arms. He carried her across the suite to a small bedroom where he laid her down gently on the bed. He considered rousing her, decided against it, and went into the other room to pour himself a drink.

The guard stood by the door, looking nervous. Ramirez handed him a glass. "Relax, Luis. It is done.

We will have much explaining to do tomorrow. There is a body to hide—and tomorrow also, I must find another assassin." He looked up at the guard. "There is nothing more for us to do tonight, Luis. I suggest you be very silent—even to our own men. Go back to your room and sleep."

The guard nodded glumly, and finished his drink.

On the ledge outside the window, Nightshade watched silently. The brutality had touched that hidden part of her emotions with a cold hand. It clutched tightly around her heart making her want to scream, to smash through the thin sheet of glass.

She remained silent, regaining control when her rage subsided.

11

Clara Weiss sat waiting in Doctor Black's luxury suite, as morning lengthened into afternoon. Shortly before 1:00 P.M., the bedroom door opened and Nightshade entered.

"Good afternoon, dear," said Clara. "I was wondering when you'd finally get up. There's coffee and breakfast on the sideboard."

Nightshade crossed the room and poured herself a cup of black coffee. Clara set her own cup down, and turned to face her.

"Now, would you care to tell me where you went in such a hurry last night?"

Nightshade finished the coffee, then poured another. Moving to the couch, she sat down beside her companion. "Last night. Yes. The man who came into the restaurant last night was Southern's murderer. I *had* to follow him." She told Clara how she tailed the two men to the bar and followed Bones to Ramirez' room. In blunt words she recounted Bones's death. Clara seemed relieved.

"You've kept your promise to Southern's widow. The man who killed him has been brought to justice—by his own kind. I'm glad it's over."

"But it's not over, Clara. This killing was part of something larger. Bones Gant was to be part of a test—a pilot program for World Transport's terrorists . . . and World Transport is but another front for *him*. Now I've lost him again. Unless . . ."

"Unless what?"

Nightshade's eyes burned. "Unless this operation goes ahead as planned. I know now how to get the information I need."

"Whatever you're suggesting is a *dangerous* game. It could cost you your life."

"I've told you before, Clara, nothing matters to me more than this. My life is not my own. Help me, Clara."

"I refuse to be a party to your destruction."

Nightshade calmly smiled. "Very well, then, I will do it alone." Her voice was cordial, almost friendly, but beneath a face of outward calm, burning fury raised Nightshade's right brow.

12

A glaring sun shone through the venetian blinds of the meeting room on the third floor balcony of the Hotel McCall. Wooden folding chairs had been arranged around a great oak table. The heat was oppressive. The air-conditioning was broken, and the room was filled with portable fans.

It was a gathering of many nations, many races—Africans, Arabs, Asians, Americans. It was exclusively male, with no one under thirty, and few over sixty. The faces were lined, hardened but slightly sensual, as if accustomed to the good things in life. The conversation was loud, coarse and cynical. These men were Ramirez's associates—the 'Board of Directors' of Terror, Inc.

Elena entered with a tray of drinks as Ramirez himself pounded on the table for silence. The men took refreshment, and languidly pulled themselves erect.

"My friends—let us be quiet for a moment."

The sound fell to a grudging silence.

"Thank you. If we might begin . . . ?" There was a scraping of chairs. "As some of you know," Ramirez began, "the enterprise which we discussed at our last meeting has been wholeheartedly approved by the sponsoring organization. I'm sure you realize this will mean a better year for all of us, and I hope, an end to the petty squabbles we've had in the past." Here, he turned to a dark-skinned man near him.

"Along these lines, allow me to note that my good friend Ali Achmed Bakhar has reorganized his section to avoid the divisive dissension his late predecessor was so famous for. We must all make similar efforts towards *solidarity*, gentlemen. This is far too sweet an opportunity to let slip through greedy fingers.

"The one thing I feel I must caution you about before we begin planning this operation, is that our benefactors expect an efficient, *businesslike* organization. Those of you who cannot meet this standard must fear not only your opposition, but your fellows as well.

"I believe that expresses my position succinctly. Are there any questions before we continue? Yes. Identify yourself, please."

"Pak, Indochina." The speaker was a short, overweight Asian with no trace of an accent. "My delegation wants to know how we are to be paid for a successful assignment. As you know, we've had bad experiences with government funds that never showed up. What makes you think your businessmen will be any more reliable?"

Ramirez smiled, nodding. "Did you have any trouble with your transportation here, Harry?"

"No, no trouble at all."

"Passports, customs, law officers, parking tickets?"

"No problem."

"You are on expense account now, my friend. None of

this will ever trouble you again nor will any other financial matter . . . provided, of course, that you play on the team."

Another man rose. "Ntungi, Swaziland. We were absent from the previous meeting. We are wondering if you can justify our working through you. Our political ambitions seem secure at this point. What can we gain from your so-called 'organization'?"

Ramirez looked sharply at the African. "If I had known there were political motivations for your work with us, I would never have dealt with you. It is essential that every man here is above *political* considerations. We cannot hope to manipulate the fate of nations if we care too much about their *people*. I have reiterated this time and again. Whenever ideals enter into our work, we become useless. In your case, Ntungi, you may anticipate primarily a caretaker role—unless your neighbors to the north become too difficult to manage."

The African nodded and sat down.

"Yes, Ali?"

"I address this—excuse me, Ali Bahkar, Mid-East—I address this to the gathering at large. It becomes more and more obvious that our new employers will be asking us to take a role that runs counter to the interests of a great number of our countrymen. We would hope that we can count on the rest of you for support—in the form of protest, sabotage and diversion when a crucial action is necessary. I would like to ask the group for a vote on this at a later time. We will, of course, reciprocate as we can."

"Fine. If there are no objections, we'll place it on the agenda. Yes?"

"Claudio Mateo, Guatemala. My group, and I'm sure the rest of us as well, are interested in this first test project, the 'Carib' operation. Since the arrangement depends on its success, we would like to know a bit more about it. A progress report, so to speak."

Ramirez looked intently at the young man, his hands clasped tightly behind his back as he replied: "We have decided, among ourselves, that 'Carib' must be undertaken with extremely close security measures. For this reason, I would prefer not to go into it further with the group at large. Those directly involved will be briefed further during the planning sessions. Upon its completion, a full summary of 'Carib' will be given. Now, are there any further questions? No? Then let's get down to business."

* * *

By sunset, many of the participants had tired of the details of the new enterprise and were willing to leave minutiae of the program to their colleagues. Several sat on the Spanish-style balcony, laughing and watching traffic. One or two had drifted down the hall. Ramirez sat with two or three more active members, gesturing to a stack of papers and hammering home a point. Suddenly there was a clamor in the hall. A figure burst in, pursued by two heavyset bodyguards.

The intruder's face was lit by the amber rays of the dying sun. She was incredibly tall, and the effect was heightened by a mass of wiry black hair shot with white streaks that gave her a macabre aspect. She was dressed in black military fatigues, and a necklace of teeth hung at her throat. Her skin was brown and her nails and lips were black. Her face was hideously gorgeous, like a famous beauty gone mad. Her right eye sparkled with a demonic fire—her left was covered by a black patch, on which was painted a glaring crimson eye. Although she wore an empty cartridge belt, she had no gun. A large hunting knife hung at her hip.

She started toward Ramirez, and one of the guards grabbed her arm. She twisted his arm behind him, forcing him to his knees. The other drew his gun. She re-

leased the guard. "Peace! I am looking for Carl Ramirez." Her voice was husky and deep. Carl turned and was held by her gaze as the guard lowered his gun. He smiled. "I am Ramirez. Whom have I the pleasure of addressing?"

The men in the room turned to watch the pair. She moved a few steps closer. "I am Marie Therese St. Jacques. My friends and enemies alike know me as *Mama Dimanche*."

Ramirez stiffened. One or two more heads turned.

"What can I do for you, Señora?" He eyed her warily.

"A few moments only of your time, someplace private?" Her face contorted in a sensuous parody of a lewd expression, her tongue wetting her lips. Carl felt a chill creep up his back. He scanned the group, then took her arm. Her skin was icy.

"Come with me. Excuse me, gentlemen. I will be a moment."

A guard volunteered to accompany him.

"No, thank you, Raoul. I know how to handle myself, with a woman." He escorted her into a small antechamber, closing the door and drawing her close.

"Now, what in the name of all that is holy is this about? Who in hell are you?"

"Surely you remember me, Carl. Our paths crossed once before—in Santo Domingo. I was one of your best customers for those shiny new American rifles you used to sell."

"Dimanche . . . Dimanche . . ." As Ramirez studied the bizarre costume, a beat of recognition arched its way to his brow. "Dimanche . . . but this is impossible! The woman called Mama Dimanche was killed by government forces over five years ago. The *Président*'s men bragged how they plucked out her eye for a trophy. I have even seen it!"

The woman smiled a ghastly grin.

"It is hard to kill a witch-woman, Carl. As for the eye

. . ." She lifted her patch. A shriveled socket was visible beneath. "It will be mine again!"

"What are you here for?"

"I come for business. You are in need of an experienced executioner, one who knows the islands—*non*?"

Ramirez's jaw tensed.

"I have one."

"Come, Carl, let us not play games with one another. I watched your lily-white torpedo leave this morning with the rest of the soiled linen. Tell me, do I meet your specifications?"

"I need a killer."

"And what am I? Did Mama Dimanche not kill Ministre LaVache in his bed in the Palace, while all slept? And what of that young Colonel who wanted to be boss of all of Santo Domingo? He died as well, did he not?"

Ramirez felt the chill again. Colonel Garcia, of whom she spoke, had become a burden to the Dominican President, and Ramirez was hired to exterminate him. Garcia was found garrotted, and Ramirez took credit for the assassination. He spoke to no one, save his most trusted lieutenants, of the strange circumstances of the death, which bore all the traces of a ritual voodoo murder. He long suspected the work was done by the mysterious Mama Dimanche. How could this intruder know of it, unless it was actually her? If Mama Dimanche still lived, she could prove a formidable ally.

"Let us for the moment accept that you are who you say you are. What do you hope to get out of this?"

"Two things, Carl. The first should be obvious: Money. Then, I would like a comfortable post in the new government—say, Minister of Wild Life. These have been lean years, and I long to eat well again. And my signs say you have found the pot of gold, eh, Carl? Your new work agrees with you. Well, I would have a piece. I will pay my way, a fair exchange. He dies, your marionette comes to power, and I have a pretty house and a few pennies for my old age. Payment upon delivery—an ear, perhaps? His golden skull ring? You have only to ask."

"This is madness. You have no idea what is at stake. It is ridiculous, preposterous. I will hear no more!"

"As you will, Carl. But you realize you have very little choice. You can't keep that hired killer's death a secret for long. I found out. So can others. Admit it, I'm the best offer you've had all day!" She winked broadly.

Ramirez sighed deeply. The group he was dealing with was a volatile one. There were important matters to be arranged, and little time to waste. And now this woman had complicated things. If word were to leak out on Bones's death, his whole scheme could be jeopardized before he had a chance to operate.

He rose quickly, opened the door and took the strange woman with him. "Clearly, Madame, you have given me much to think about. We will discuss this proposition of yours further, in the morning. For the present, however, I must ask that you remain here—as my guest, of course."

"Afraid I'll spill it, man? I've got my price."

They arrived at the door of a small room down the hall. Ramirez opened it with his own key. "Please, make yourself at home. Good night, Madame."

"*Bo'soir*, Carl." She winked again. "Pleasant dreams." The door closed, and Ramirez locked it with his key. He whistled. A guard came quickly.

"See that the lady is not disturbed, that no one enters or leaves. Understood?"

"Yes, sir."

Ramirez was met by one of his men at the entrance to the conference room.

"There you are, Carl. The men are restless and talking about breaking up for the night. What happened? Who was that crazy woman?"

"A former business associate. She wanted to talk over old times."

The man smiled, and nudged him in the side.

"*Business* associate—I get it, right!" He grinned wider.

"Come on," said Ramirez curtly, "let's get this over with."

13

Carl Ramirez sat up in bed, sipping a stale whiskey, and smoking a slim cigar. His brain whirled furiously over what the coming day would bring. The tan back and flank of his woman was half revealed by the lemon sheet that covered her. The tang of her body drifted subtly in the air. He snapped out the light, stubbed out the *cigarillo*, and glared at the dial of the alarm clock. It was almost midnight. He twisted over and set it for six. He punched the pillow, mumbling an automatic *ave maria* under his breath as he did every night of his life, and rolled against Elena's soft body.

Something moved in the darkness. Carl sprung erect. Quickly, his eyes searched the shadows until . . .

There! In the corner of the room, nearly five feet off the ground, a glaring crimson eye was floating towards him! Carl instantly told himself that it was his imagina-

tion, that it was a trick ... But now, what was that sound?

"Carlos!"

"Elena?" No! She was asleep, but he had heard a woman's voice.

"Carrrrlossss!" A face! Now a body! Was it *she, Mama Dimanche*?

Then it was flesh and blood, a woman, half in shadow. Ramirez felt foolish and bewildered. He shouted. "How in hell did you get in here, you old wolf-bitch?"

"Quiet!" she whispered. "You'll wake your pretty kitten."

"What do you want, Dimanche?"

"Then you accept that it is I. Now we have business to talk, Ramirez."

Carl growled, feeling less bold than he appeared. She had gotten free!

"Very well, you will *have* your answer. Tomorrow.

Now go. Turn into a bat and fly out of here for all I care. Trouble no more the sleep of decent men!" The witch woman cackled, but turned to go, her body again becoming faint.

"Very well, Carlos . . . Tomorrow it will be."

Ramirez closed his eyes for a moment to shake the sleep from them, but the woman had vanished. He cursed under his breath, said another *ave maria*, then turned over for a fitful slumber filled with strange and disquieting dreams.

* * *

The alarm shrieked. A hand fumbled for the button and shut it off.

Carl Ramirez had a very bad night. As he struggled up from sleep the image of Mama Dimanche was still with him. His mouth felt like moldering leather.

He leaned over, swatting Elena on the rump, and swung his feet to the floor. As she awoke, he growled a single word—"coffee." She grabbed her robe and rushed to the hot-plate. This was obviously not a morning to argue.

Ramirez sat on the edge of the bed, trying to wake up. Suddenly the phone beside the bed rang shrill. He swore.

The insistent ringing continued, and he grudgingly picked up the receiver.

"Yes?"

"Ramirez? This is Hunter."

"I am in no mood to talk to you. Make it short."

"I think, Mr. Ramirez, that you would be wise to meet with me immediately. I have been informed that the delivery I made to you has been . . . damaged. Do you follow me?"

Ramirez groaned. It was not so much that Hunter found out about Bones, but that he was being his usual damn-fool self at six o'clock in the morning.

"What do you want?"

"I will expect you at check-point six in one hour. I assume you will take all necessary precautions." The line went dead, and Ramirez cursed Hunter's stupid cloak-and-dagger mentality. He toyed with the idea of not going, but Hunter meant Winston, and Winston was paying the bills. There was no putting it off any longer.

* * *

A blue 1966 Dodge station wagon pulled up at a roadside rest on the Rickenbacker causeway to Key Biscayne. A short middle-aged man in white bermuda shorts, dark blue shirt, and a sky blue fishing cap unloaded tackle. He baited his hook and cast it into the placid water.

A few minutes later, a red convertible Mustang pulled up next to the Dodge. A lean, tanned man got out and sat down at one of the picnic tables. The fisherman started to search his pockets in an exaggerated fashion, cursed loudly, and walked over to the table.

"Got a light, mister?"

"Oh, for heaven's sake, Hunter, shove it. There's no one else within miles of us at this hour of the morning!"

"This is no game, Ramirez, although you seem to think it is. Give me the proper counter-sign."

"I'M-SORRY-MY-LIGHTER-IS-OUT-OF-FUEL. Now, can we get down to business?"

"I received an anonymous tip that Bones was killed. Mr. Winston is extremely angry."

"And how the hell does *he* know?"

"I know my duty. I informed him this morning. He wishes to meet with you this afternoon."

"I can't leave Miami today!"

"Mr. Winston will be here by two o'clock."

Ramirez was silent for a moment, his mind working frantically. Winston was ugly when he was angry. There must be some way to pull this mess, not to mention his own ass, out of the fire. His eyes narrowed. That crazy woman, Mama Dimanche, might be the answer, but he'd have to play it right.

Ramirez fixed Hunter with what he hoped was a convincing look.

"Hunter, listen carefully. Bones was forced on us by Winston. He would've ruined the entire operation. Now that he's dead, we have half a chance of pulling it off."

"What do you mean, 'half a chance'? Bones was a skilled assassin."

"Bones was a hired gun. He didn't care who he hit, as long as the pay was good and he got out with his skin.

"Suppose I could provide an agent who knows the islands," Ramirez continued, "an agent who hates the *Président* with a passion, and will do anything to see him dead—even risking her life in a suicide mission?"

Hunter broke in, "*Her* life? You mean, you would entrust a critical mission like this to a woman? For such an important task, only a *man* has the strength and courage, the honor!"

Ramirez smiled. It was working.

"This woman was one of the finest *guerrilla* leaders in the islands. She commanded blind, obedient loyalty from her troops. She can out-shoot, out-fight, and out-maneuver any man you can name. Have you heard of *Mama Dimanche*?"

"You're mad. Winston will certainly have to hear about this."

"Splendid. Tell your Mr. Winston that I will present my assassin for his approval today, at his meeting."

Ramirez strode to his car, slammed the door. As he sped down the causeway, he congratulated himself on his skillful use of a stroke of good fortune.

Hunter's eyes followed the rapidly disappearing car. Ramirez *was* a fool—he was sure of it now. *Mama Dimanche*. Hunter knew that woman was dead. The spy shook his head and cast his line back into the water. Mr. Winston would know what to do.

14

Edward Winston sat fuming behind a desk in the "Presidential Suite" of the Hotel McCall. Hunter had just finished a report of his meeting with Ramirez, and had given him a dossier on this "Mama Dimanche". The whole 'Carib' operation seemed in jeopardy.

"Get out of here, Hunter. When they arrive, tell Ramirez I want to see him alone. You wait outside with this woman. Is that understood?"

"Yes, sir."

Winston pulled the dossier across the desk. There were no photographs, in fact the report said it was believed she cast no reflection or shadow. There was, however, an artist's sketch of the woman as she was known by a comrade during previous activities on the island. There was also a snapshot of a small specimen jar with a dark brown eye floating in it. Written in French and English on the back was a date and the name *Mama Dimanche*.

By all accounts she was a professional. Winston did not believe in the sorcery she was said to practice, but clearly the peasants did, and that could be an asset. The list of her suspected victims read like an honor roll in a VFW hall. She could prove a competent assassin, despite the loose ends. Winston respected quality. Something, however, was suspicious about this. Winston was determined to find out what it was before he was to meet this unexpected visitor.

There was a knock at the door.

Hunter looked in. "Ramirez is here, sir."

Ramirez was having second thoughts about this meeting. Mama Dimanche had appeared for the meeting, not as an avenging ghost, but looking almost human. She dressed in a severe black pantsuit, and seemed younger, although the lines still showed about her neck and eyes. She wore no patch, and her crazy mane of hair was pulled back into a ponytail, tied with a grey ribbon. She looked more like a businesswoman than a voodoo witch and hardened assassin.

Hunter fidgeted by the elevator, watching her reflection in the curved mirror, like a two-bit spy. She turned to stare at him and he coughed. He leaned casually against the wall and began to whistle in a monotone.

Ramirez entered Winston's quarters alone, advancing to shake hands with him.

"Mr. Winston, good to see you again."

"Sit down, Ramirez. You've come pretty damn close to sabotaging a multi-million dollar operation. You better have a good story. I have no patience with stupidity. You're just as expendable as Bones was, Carl."

"Mr. Winston, Bones was an extremely poor choice for this task. He was not familiar with the island, or the people—he did not even speak the dialect. He was simply a hired gunman, nothing more."

"So now you present me with this creature to make up

for your own bungling. Is that right, Ramirez?"

"Mr. Winston, there can be no doubt that this woman would be the best possible agent. If I had known before that she was alive. . ."

"Yes, Ramirez, *if* you had known. The problem is that *all* my sources say Mama Dimanche is *dead*. Do you expect me to take this woman on *faith*?" Winston's voice rose in anger.

"Sir, she is *alive*, and she is *here*. Forgive me for my bluntness, but I will take *full responsibility* for this agent. If you wish the support of my organization, you *must* agree. May I suggest that you at least meet her before you make a decision?"

Winston scratched the back of his head. ". . .Very well, Carl. Bring in this reanimated witch and Hunter too."

Ramirez went to the door. Winston wasn't accepting anything, and the situation was explosive. This trump card better come through.

"Come in. Both of you."

Hunter and Mama Dimanche hesitated for a moment, each awaiting the other's move. Finally, the woman strode forward through the door. Hunter followed.

As they entered, Winston looked up from his papers.

"Close the door behind you, Hunter."

There was one other chair in the room besides Winston's. Ramirez stood by the window . . . Hunter leaned against the wall. The tall woman relaxed in the chair, her arms folded.

"Madame. . .?"

She bowed ironically. "Mr. Winston."

"Madame, what can I do for you?"

"First, you may tell the young man with the machine gun behind that door to lower it. It might go off and hurt someone."

Winston raised an eyebrow. "Kurt, do as the lady wishes."

"Next, I would like to know how much you were

105

prepared to pay Mr. Gant to undertake this contract."

"A reasonable request for a potential applicant, but I must decline to answer. Certain assurances are required first. How do I know you are capable of carrying out this assignment?"

"You obviously know my record. May I add that the sketch in that dossier is not entirely accurate?"

Winston rubbed the side of his head. "I know the record of *Marie Therese St. Jacques. Her* body was interred with those of several other insurgents in a pit outside the Citadel. Her eye was plucked out. All this has been verified to my satisfaction. Do you still claim to be this woman?"

"I am Mama Dimanche."

"You might be a spy or ... an impostor."

The woman reached up to her eye and plucked it out. Winston remained unmoved. She replaced it.

"How did you survive? Or would you have me believe that you did *not*? That you are *dead*?"

"I can say only the truth. Here is the bullet that slew me."

She moved her blouse to show a bullet on a chain.

"It struck me above the heart, *here*!"

She opened her blouse slightly to reveal a dark hole. It was covered with scar tissue, obviously an old wound. Winston watched undisturbed.

"I see you are a pragmatist, M'sieur Winston. Let me give you proof, then. Feel my heartbeat!" She moved forward and grabbed his wrist. She pulled it against her chest and held it there for a moment. Then she touched his hand to her throat. He could detect no pulse. Winston frowned.

"That is indeed a remarkable feat, Madame, very effective for fooling peasants or ignorant men. But I'm afraid it will not do. I require positive proof. Kurt, Alfredo! Take custody of this woman."

Two massive men, armed with machine guns, marched

into the room. The first gestured for her to rise. Dimanche launched herself at them, slamming her fist into the throat of one gunman. As he fell, she wrenched the gun from his hands, and pushed the butt into the base of his skull. Then she swiveled, covering the other gunman. She ordered him to drop his weapon. He stood unmoving.

Dimanche swung the weapon at Winston. He nodded to the man, and Alfredo lowered his gun to the floor. The woman walked to the desk and laid the weapon in front of Winston. He looked at her, a slight smile about his lips. He shook his head as he gazed at the crumpled form on the floor. "Pardon me, Madame. You are a professional. You didn't. . ."

"Kill him? Of course not. It would be a terrible waste to do so. I hope they don't try to detain me again."

"I'm sorry—you know far too much to be allowed to leave."

Winston pulled an automatic from his desk. Dimanche feinted. He fired, and the woman doubled over, clutching her stomach.

Slowly she straightened, with blood trickling from her belly. She held out the bloody flattened bullet, then threw it down on the desk, spat, and turned to leave.

"Wait. . ."

The woman turned slowly to face Winston.

"Yes?"

"Sit down, Madame."

Winston shook his head, smiling at Hunter and Ramirez.

"Hunter, do you still say that this woman is useless? I think perhaps she will do."

Hunter's mouth moved, but he could not speak.

"Ramirez?"

"I am convinced, sir, more than ever. I believe her to be the best choice in the present situation."

"I am inclined to agree. Madame, your power of

suggestion is extraordinary. What is your secret? Hypnosis?"

"I have told you I am a witch, a practitioner of Old Ways. Is that not enough for you?"

"I don't like dealing with unknown quantities."

"A pity."

"You are obviously superbly trained, well educated. You disarmed two of my best guards, and you have the means to resist gunfire. Such talent does not go unnoticed."

"Or unrewarded. . .?"

"I·have little choice. This operation cannot afford to be delayed."

Dimanche came right to the point. "My sources indicate that you offered Mr. Gant one hundred thousand dollars for the contract."

"Two hundred, actually. Fifty before, fifty after, and ten a year for the next ten years."

"You are a generous man."

"It is a dangerous mission."

"I have never hesitated at danger, M'sieur Winston."

"So I see. I believe we can discuss business, Madame. Hunter, Ramirez, if you would be good enough to give the lady some of the details. . . Alfredo! Bring some chairs."

* * *

The elderly desk clerk looked up in astonishment when the elevator door opened. He had just arrived for night duty, and the darkened lobby wasn't yet lit. Emerging from the car was a dark-skinned woman with a wild gleam in her eye.

Mama Dimanche saw the man staring at her, and threw him a horrible grin. He quickly lowered his head and busied himself with polishing the gold-rimmed spectacles which so seldom adorned his nose.

Quickly, gracefully, she strode out into the Miami twilight. The heat was palpable and the sky was a dark blue as she crossed the street to the park by the water. Park lamps began to flicker tentatively as Mama Dimanche disappeared from view between a building and a clump of shrubs.

She pulled a black bag from behind a trash can and withdrew a small bottle and a cloth. Wetting the cloth, she wiped it across the back of her hand, exposing a streak of pale skin against the tan.

Her fingers flew, removing the wig, facial putty and lenses to stow them into the bag. As darkness fell, Nightshade stepped into the harsh glare of the lights and was gone.

15

The dressing room of the Albemarle was dimly lit. A woman sat in a satin robe taking stage makeup off her face. Doctor Black had broken all attendance records for the hotel the previous week, and tonight Aaron Meyer was forced to turn away over a hundred people.

The performance had been flawless. Wade Beaumont had volunteered from the audience, presumably to reestablish the friendship so rudely broken off by her departure a few nights earlier. He had consented to be forced into a tiny box and had vanished under a cloth.

When the act was over, he found himself standing backstage. Patiently, he waited for Doctor Black's final curtain. When she greeted him, it was evident that fatigue was her true suitor, but so insistent a figure as Wade Beaumont would not be put off by a gracious smile.

Poor man. He would find himself, fully clothed, swimming laps around the hotel pool to cool off his ardour. At the thought of Beaumont dripping wet and bewildered, Doctor Black was almost amused, but then her face settled into an impassive mask, as if the identities of Nightshade and Doctor Black had found a balance in this expression. The meeting with Edward Winston left her bitterly disappointed. The phrase that had cut deep into her was an innocuous one. It should not have affected her so.

He explained what he wanted her to do. He gave her instructions and papers, and ordered her retainer. Then he had excused himself, saying: "I'll only be a moment. I have to get this confirmed."

I have to get this confirmed.

Confirmed? By whom?

She had woven her net tightly. Each aspect of her plan had been carefully calculated. When the end came, *he* would know *why* and *how* it had come.

Yet Winston's decision to hire the mysterious Mama Dimanche had to be *confirmed*. What *else* had to be confirmed? **Was the man she sought about to escape again?**

With a photographic clarity, she recalled the faces of the men who had led her at last to Edward Winston. Each one, in turn, had pointed a finger upward, ever upward. And now, when she seemed to have reached the top, something must be *confirmed*.

She swore coldly. A thousand horrible damnations on these men with their faceless pyramidal hierarchies! Whose hand pulled Edward Winston's strings? What sort of being could order about the President of one of the largest multinational corporations in the world? Someone, somewhere played with the lives of millions of people as if they were toys.

She composed herself then and closing her eyes, she repeated the vow made on the night she finally realized who she was. She would have to continue to play the game, make herself worthy of notice.

Perhaps this time he had betrayed himself. This was the organization in which she saw most clearly his hand at work. It must be his favorite plaything.

An unnamed instinct told her to pursue the thought. What would he do if his big, expensive toy were to be broken—crumbled before his eyes? With icy determination, she shook herself from her reverie. There was work to be done.

* * *

Nightshade sat alone in the hotel suite, blinds closed to the late morning sun, listening to a cassette player, repeating the words. A male voice intoned phrases in a language that sounded almost like French, but with a strange cadence. She repeated the phrases exactly, intent on the subtle intonations. When the tape reached its end, she rewound it for the seventh time, and began again.

Clara Weiss entered from the hallway, seeing her friend surrounded by a pile of books, maps and tapes. She was about to turn on the light, but hesitated, unwilling to disturb her. But Nightshade turned, pressing the stop button, and looked up.

"Were you able to find it?"

"Yes," Clara answered, "in a little bookstore on the other side of town."

The older woman tossed a battered black book with the word *Vodun* lettered in red on the spine, onto the pile of books and papers.

"There. It cost a small fortune, but it's the genuine article."

"Thank you, Clara. Thank you for everything, for helping me this way."

Clara settled next to her. "I don't suppose there's any sense in trying to talk you out of this."

"No, Clara. All my life, my every action has been leading up to this. If I turn aside now, it will all have been wasted."

"Do you realize what a gamble you're taking?"

"What do you mean?"

"Consider what you're planning for a moment. In order to find the man you seek, you will have to play the part of a hardened assassin. You may be forced to prove yourself." Clara took a deep breath. "If you won't think of your own life, at least think of the lives of innocent people who may be hurt. Is it worth the risk?"

"It's a risk I have to take, Clara."

Clara Weiss sat for long moments, silent. Then she rose, crossing to her handbag, which rested by the door. She opened it, returning with a small amber bottle. She placed it in Nightshade's hand.

"What's this, Clara?"

"Tri-melanolic acid. Taken internally, it darkens the skin. Unless counteracted, the effects last up to six months.

Clara crossed to the door to the room, then paused. "You're determined to be a *fool*, but there's no need to be ignorant at the same time. It would be ironic if Mama. Dimanche were betrayed by *herself*."

The door closed, leaving Nightshade in darkness. For several minutes, she sat silently in thought. Then her hand reached for the recorder.

Then her hand reached for the recorder.

16

A warm breeze swept around the corner of the McCall Hotel, carrying a newspaper with it. Carl Ramirez, his arms and chest bare, walked from the shade into the gathering heat. As the light changed, he crossed to the cracked, pale pink facade of the hotel. He glanced at his watch. It was nearly seven.

He pushed through the revolving door into the coolness of the lobby. Three men sat waiting. One, a large brooding Latin with a thick moustache, rose as Ramirez entered, his soft posture becoming military. The other two men were black, one slim and tall, the other short and thickly built.

"Have Hunter's men arrived yet?" asked Ramirez.

"Hunter called a couple of minutes ago," replied the Latin. "He said he would meet us in the briefing room at seven-thirty."

"Good. Let's get started."

The "briefing room" was a portion of the hotel basement once used to store supplies for the ground-floor restaurant during its more affluent days. The room had been cleared, and a small wooden podium stood near one wall before a small semi-circle of chairs.

The Latin turned on the lights. The tall black man took a sheaf of papers from a side table and carried it up to the lectern. He glanced at his notes and looked up.

"Carl, who is this new assassin you've found? I could get nothing from Ramos on the way from the airport." He jerked his thumb at the Latin.

"Be patient, Henri. I promise you she will be worth waiting for."

Henri raised an eyebrow. "A woman, Carl? You are not letting some personal matter cloud your usual good judgement, are you?" His words were languid, richly toned with a Creole accent.

"You will see for yourself soon, my friend."

Henri Boyette, Haitian-born, was one of Carl Ramirez's chief lieutenants. He had spent the last ten years in the service of various South American governments. Although he was in his late thirties, he appeared younger. His jaw was soft, and his mouth was petulant. His suave manners and thick accent often led people to underestimate him, but a cool fire in his great brown eyes hinted at a cruel and logical mind. Today he was dressed flamboyantly in purple. His satin shirt, open to the third button, showed a length of gold chain against the dark chest.

Boyette's companion was Ira Cain, a former Special Forces commando trained in counterinsurgency. His appearance was a total contrast to Boyette's. He was squat and muscular, with a full beard and hair. He was dressed in jeans, a khaki T-shirt, and an old denim hat.

Esteban Ramos was the representative of Moses Cruz, the mulatto Dominican General upon whom the success of the Carib operation depended. Ramos had displayed a keen talent for military strategy while fighting alongside Ramirez in the Dominican peasant uprisings several years before. In the heat of battle, Ramos was cool and professional. But Ramirez had also seen him when the battle was won, and found him a grossly sensual man who took his pleasure where he found it and was among the first to claim the spoils.

Harold Hunter arrived punctually. Two men followed him into the room. The first was introduced as Manuel Martinez, Hunter's specialist on munitions and demolition. Ramirez knew him only by reputation. He had participated in many Caribbean escapades by Western governments over the past two decades. Graying now and heavily tanned, he might be able to pass as one of the mulatto farmers who eke a living from the small coffee plantings along the border.

The second man was white and an American. His name was Carter. He was, so Hunter said, a skilled pilot of both air and water craft. It appeared that Hunter had again filled the request for a specialist without thought as to how he would fit into the mission. Perhaps the full beard he had grown and his comparative youth would persuade the locals that he was an American radical. Ramirez was doubtful, but he must take what he was given. He had disobeyed Winston's orders once; he did not dare attempt it again.

The men helped themselves to cigars and coffee and settled themselves in the chairs. Ramirez's watch read nearly eight. If his assassin, Mama Dimanche, arrived as planned, he could begin to forge a strikeforce.

Promptly at eight she arrived. Heads swiveled to watch as she entered. She was dressed in a tan jumpsuit, her muscular brown arms bare. Her one eye met theirs.

"*Madre de dios!*" Ramos swore softly. Boyette looked sharply at Ramirez. Ramirez introduced the men by name and gestured to a seat in the front row.

"Please be seated, Madame. Gentlemen, may I present

117

our expert in extermination, Marie Therese St. Jacques. Some of you may know her better by her *nom de guerre*—Mama Dimanche."

"Is this true, Carl?" asked Ramos, "I had thought this she-witch was slain years ago by the *M'sieur le Président*'s werewolf squad, his *loups garous*!"

"It is true. Quite a catch, eh, Esteban?"

"If it is indeed she, yes." He turned, leaning over his chair, to the rest of the men. "This lady gave both the *Président* and my own men a hard time for many months. I hope you will not be offended, Señora, if I say that I breathed easier when I heard you had finally been run to ground."

"Not at all, M'sieur Ramos," Mama Dimanche laughed, "I consider it a great compliment."

Henri Boyette examined her intently, saying, "I am sure all of us would be interested in how you accomplished your escape from *M'sieur le Président*'s troops, how you come to be alive today. It must be quite a tale."

She returned the Haitian's dark stare.

"Very well, I will tell you. But some of what I say will sound strange—especially to the Americans. First, I must explain a little about *vodun*, or voodoo as it is called. It is no game of party dancing and chicken slaying, but an old religion that black men and women brought with them on the slave boats. We worship the old gods and goddesses, the *loa* or *mystéres*, and they look out for us.

"My own *mait' tete*, my mistress, is *Aida Wedo* wife of *Damballa*, prince of the *loa*. It was she who made me a *mambo bocur*, a witch priestess, and it was she who protected me from the *Président* and his men."

Carter choked back a derisive laugh. "You don't expect us to believe that garbage, do you?"

"Do not mock what you have not seen, young man," she replied. "Even the *Président* himself believes in *vodun*. When he came to power, he called the most powerful *mambos* and *houngans* to his side. Those who came with him are fat and have fine houses in the city. Those of us who would not serve him he tracked down, one by one. He called powerful *loa bossals*, wild spirits down on us. Those who opposed him are now sick, or dead, or hiding in the hills.

"Finally they captured me as well, after I had slain the *Président*'s favorite minister while he slept. They made a great production of the execution. *M'sieur le Président* himself turned out to see it. They even had a priest charm a silver bullet for me." She smiled. "But it is no great thing for a daughter of *Aida Wedo* to resist gunfire. If you doubt me, ask M'sieur Hunter. He has seen it himself."

Hunter objected, "It was a trick!"

"Trick or no, it served. I fell as dead. But I did not die. I had taken an herb of which I was given *connaissance* by Mama *Aida Wedo*. I slept. And while I slept, those bastards stole my eye!"

As she continued, a strange and compelling quality filled her words. "I awoke at the dark of the moon in a wood box, in the dirt. I dug myself out. Hiding and stealing, I made my way to the house of friends, who saw me safely out of the country."

But Boyette shook off the spell. "Let us assume what you say is true, Madame. Where have you been all this time? Why do you now return?"

"I have been with my sister's family in Trinidad, M'sieur Boyette. I have been licking my wounds and praying for the *Président*'s death. As for why I have returned, it is simple. You have a plan to put a man in power who will give my people roads and light and water. I know these people, their ways are mine. I wish to help you."

Boyette laughed sharply. "Can *that* be your only reason, Madame? What we propose to do will probably leave the people just as miserable as before, if not worse. Instead of a black tyrant, there will be a brown tyrant, that is all. And they will be forced to turn over to the government their little plots of land of which they are so proud, and to work for slave wages growing sugar for Americans to have on their breakfast cereal. Perhaps your reasons are more selfish, eh?"

For a moment she regarded him with a cold stare, then she smiled. "What you say has truth, M'sieur Boyette. I am no fool who thinks to have a saint in the palace, but anyone would be better than the monster who sits there now—and, if putting your man in power brings me a little personal fortune, who am I to refuse?" She turned to Ramirez. "Carl, you will vouch for me with these skeptics, *non*? If not, I fear I am wasting my time."

"My friends," said Ramirez, "I am convinced that she speaks the truth. But more important, Mr. Winston of World Transport believes in her. Surely *that* is enough. Come, let us get down to business. We have much to do today. Henri, since you will be leading the assault, perhaps you could review the mission for us."

Boyette rose and crossed to the podium.

"Thank you, Carl. Mr. Hunter will remain in Miami to keep in contact with our clients. Mr. Ramirez will accompany us to the base camp in Santo Domingo, and remain in radio contact with us. The rest is up to us.

"Briefly then, here is our mission. World Transport Enterprises, which has extensive holdings in the Dominican Republic, wishes to extend its influence into Haiti. They have a profitable relationship with the Santo Domingo government, providing arms and capital in exchange for favorable trade concessions. They have been unable to make similar arrangements in Haiti because of the stubborn and capricious character of the *Président*. There have been several attempts to reason with him, but each has met with failure. That leaves force.

"There is an additional obstacle. An emerging leftist

faction in the government has been growing stronger. Until recently there has been no strong leader among them who dared oppose the *Président*'s rule. But a year ago, Ulysse Follette, son of a beloved Cabinet Minister exterminated under the old regime, an avowed Marxist, returned from exile. He has encamped among the ragged *marrons* or hill bandits near thev border, and has begun to gain support among the peasants.

"The coalition which could form under Follette between the peasants and the intellectuals is an even greater threat to World Transport. A popular uprising could drive free enterprise from Haiti and in time could infect the Dominicans as well.

"We must therefore perform *two* functions for World Transport: installing a government more willing to bargain with them, and ridding the country of its leftist influences. And, we must accomplish this so that neither World Transport nor any government can be implicated in what must appear to be a national movement toward self-determination.

"We will accomplish this by arranging for Dominican forces to enter the Haitian capital on the pretext of suppressing a Communist threat. Since no such threat exists at present, we must create one. We must join forces with Follette, and persuade him to raise a peasant army for a great assault on the capital. In the confusion resulting from our entry into the city, an assassin will have the opportunity to reach the *Président*.

"With the *Président* dead and the city in chaos, Ramos will contact General Cruz of the Dominican Army. He will swiftly cross the border into Port-au-Prince and put down the "Communist Revolution." Once in power, he will declare a new "government of the people" which will act in coordination with the Dominican government to impose a single rule on the island." He scanned the group. "Any questions? *Bon.* Our plane will leave from the airport tomorrow morning for Santo Domingo. We should be making the jump into the Haitian hill country within forty-eight hours." Boyette gathered his papers and returned to his chair.

"Thank you, Henri," said Carl Ramirez. "Before we continue I wish to stress two things. First, although General Cruz has agreed to support our effort one hundred percent, he cannot act without provoking an international incident, until the threat of a major political uprising actually exists. I must also caution you not to forget the interests of those who made this possible. They are expecting above all a careful, efficient service for their money. If they are disappointed, they will be swift and merciless in their retribution. There is much more at stake here than a single mission. You would be wise to remember that."

17

Clara Weiss paused as she passed the darkened room of the Greenwich Village brownstone. A cluster of cosmetics were scattered carelessly in front of the great mirror, but the rest of the room pulsed with a monastic sparseness.

She moved almost automatically into the room, adjusting the clutter. As she raised her head, her eyes were caught by a photograph on the wall, reflected in the mirror.

It was a young woman with glossy raven hair pulled back, dressed in evening garb, producing a snow-white dove from a top hat. To an unfamiliar eye, it could have been a recent dress portrait of Doctor Black at Carnegie Hall.

But a closer look revealed small incongruous details: the quaint formal attire of a man in the first row, the antique style of the floodlights, and a great spidery inscription in a flowing hand—*"Lili Black, Berlin, 1939."*

Clara gazed at it for a moment, a sad smile gracing her lips. Then she averted her gaze. Those days were over. There was a new Doctor Black now—young, facile, capable.

As her thoughts returned again to her young charge, she bit her lip unconsciously, remembering the charred, catatonic thing she had rescued from death that dark night so long ago. For a time it seemed that the girl had been set on a new path full of high promise. Yet now there was the woman who called herself Nightshade. Was it possible to save her from her own destructiveness if she insisted on certain death so recklessly time and again?

The photograph on the wall seemed to smile knowingly at Clara. *Those* days—those reckless days when the world paused on the brink of a world war to forget its troubles in brassy cabarets—had she herself not flirted with death in those days?

Clara sighed. She was acting as if Nightshade were her daughter. In a way, the instinct was correct, but another part of her senses warned against interference. Clara remembered the lessons she had learned during the war . . . lessons that had been dearly bought . . . valuable and indelible for the price she paid.

If Nightshade were to have her confrontation with the man who had totally ruined her life—if she were to come through her pain and emerge from it whole—she would be tempered in a fire which would make her unbreakable. Yet Clara knew her namesake was being devoured by a passion of her own making, that any acts bred out of Nightshade's thirst for revenge would put both her life and sanity in jeopardy.

Clara gazed again at the photo of herself, of Doctor Black. Placing one more lid on one more jar, she turned and left the darkened room, silently praying that Night-

shade would return safely by her own will.

***

Nightshade stood alone in the hotel room, staring out at the current of life that flowed past her window. There was an irony in their ant-like, mindless purposefulness. They did not realize that within this shabby hotel a handful of men plotted the destinites of millions of people.

She felt a cold triumph growing in her. Clara would have been proud of her performance tonight. She had not only portrayed but—*became* Mama Dimanche so successfully that these men had accepted her at face value.

But it was not enough. She must use her new-found advantage to draw attention to herself, to provoke the inevitable confrontation which must one day come. Without the one thing she truly craved, all her accomplishments were nothing but ashes.

Sunrise found her still standing by the window, gazing without seeing, at the dawning day.

18

The team met for breakfast in a coffee shop near the hotel. Ramirez, Boyette and Cain, and the woman called Mama Dimanche sat at one table—Ramos, Hunter and his men at the next.

Hunter had arrived in a green panel truck with *Ace Florists* stenciled on the side. Hunter said it was their "cover" for the trip to the airport.

The day had dawned hot. The sun was unremittingly bright, and the sea breezes did little to relieve the heat. As the check was paid, Hunter walked out of the coffee shop, pulling on a pair of dark glasses, and opened the side door to the windowless van. Ramos started to laugh.

"Señor Hunter, I appreciate your desire to see that no one is aware of our movements. However, I will be damned as a goat if I will submit myself to being stuffed into a hot metal box like an animal."

Hunter nodded, a knowing look in his eye. "I anticipated your request. The interior of this transport is equipped with air conditioning. You will not have to worry about the heat."

"*Grace le Bondieu!*" sighed Boyette. "Let us go."

Hunter was true to his word. With the air conditioning turned up full, it was not only impossible to hear or be heard above the din, but the passengers were bitterly cold the entire trip. Ira Cain spent the short ride cursing the little man in the front seat enjoying the breeze from the opened window.

After several wrong turns, which Hunter later explained were to shake any possible tail, the van arrived at the field. Carter was the first out, to make the safety check of the compact executive jet with the distinctive insignia of World Transport emblazoned on its side. Ramirez ensconced himself in the co-pilot's seat. The rest of the men made admiring comments about the jet's luxurious appointments. Mama Dimanche took a seat next to Cain and across from Ramos.

There was little tension among the team members over the mission. Ramos made himself comfortable, and after a few minutes had begun to snore. Soon, Cain too was nodding drowsily. She closed her own eyes, but could not sleep.

* * *

Ira Cain woke with a snort as the plane began to circle above the landing field. He had slept soundly throughout the long flight, and stretched out his thick arms in a great yawn, apologizing as an afterthought when his hands flailed past Mama Dimanche's face. He glanced out the window, noting with satisfaction the approach to the airport.

Carl Ramirez made his way back from the cockpit. He raised his voice above the whine of the engines.

"We land momentarily. I have just received confirmation from the ground. One of Winston's men will be meeting us at the field to escort us to our quarters."

Cain turned to Mama Dimanche. "I hope they've got a meal planned, I'm *hungry*!" He shouldered his pack as the light flashed. Ramirez took a seat.

Carter brought the jet to an easy landing and it taxied along a runway toward a great World Transport hangar. The team unfastened seat belts and collected their gear. They walked down the rampway into the cool humid atmosphere of the hangar. A white jeep with the WTE insignia rolled up and a young man in white jumped out. As he crossed the pavement, he smiled and extended his hand.

"Mr. Ramirez? Warren here, Gary Warren. Afternoon, Esteban." He looked at his watch. "I'm afraid we're running a little behind schedule. If you'll all pile into the jeeps, we can get going."

As the jeeps rolled out into the sunlight, Warren turned to Mama Dimanche who sat beside him.

"Mr. Winston told me there had been a change in personnel. You're going to be taking Mr. Gant's place, right? I don't believe I got your name, Miss."

"The priest named me Marie Therese Christophe St. Jacques, but you may call me Mama Dimanche. Does the name mean anything to you?"

Warren frowned intently. "No, I'm sorry, I can't say it does. It's Creole French for 'Mother Sunday,' isn't it?"

"Of course. But in Haiti it has another meaning—it is the *ti nom* of Aida Wedo. I don't suppose you know who she is?"

"Certainly. I remember the name from my cross-cultural orientation program. It may interest you to know that I came to this job from the Ethnology Bureau of the U.S. Central Intelligence Agency. One of the lesser deities of the voodoo pantheon, isn't it?"

She gave an ironic laugh. "There is much that cannot

be learned from a book, young man."

The jeeps pulled up in front of a low prefabricated building on the edge of an abandoned airstrip. It had been built as future barracks for the rapidly expanding paramilitary guard which protected the World Transport airbase. Inside were spartan cubicles with chair, desk and cot. The team stowed their gear and re-emerged into the sun.

They crossed the airstrip to a larger building that was surrounded by a high chain-link fence. They were stopped at the gate by an armed guard who checked off their names and issued them plastic badges. Another guard opened the door.

The brightly lit air-conditioned building was a relief from the late Dominican afternoon heat. Gary Warren led them to a large room which contained a circular conference table surrounded by brightly colored plastic chairs. Carl Ramirez, who had gone ahead, looked up from the table as the others entered.

"If any of you are hungry, there are sandwiches and drinks next door. The latest weather report says there's a squall line moving in from the north, so we'll have to move take-off up to 0300 hours. We have a few things to cover before we can get some rest."

Ira Cain was the first to find food. He picked up several sandwiches from the plate, and a cool beer from the refrigerator. The others followed suit. In a few minutes they had reassembled around the table.

Ramirez pulled down a great map of the island from the wall. The border between the Dominican Republic and the Republic of Haiti was marked in blue. Ramirez marked a red "X" on the map at a point on the border some thirty miles from the northern coast.

"The last reports, from a division of Haitian troops, place Ulysse Follette's men here. We will be crossing the border under cover of darkness, but I will try to place you as close to this spot as I can. Henri, you will be in command for the duration of the mission. I expect all of you to cooperate fully with him. You are to follow as closely as possible the route marked here. Be at all times aware of the prevailing political climate and do not hesitate to exploit it.

"Let me also remind you that timing is important. *Carnaval*, the biggest festival of the year, begins in only a few days. The assault on the capital should be timed to coincide with the height of festivities, while spirits are high and the streets are filled with peasants. Please also bear in mind that I will only be able to contact you at prearranged times by shortwave from the base. To have transmitting equipment constantly in operation could be fatal. A final transmission should be sent at nightfall on the evening of the assault. At my signal, General Cruz will approach the border of Belladere. You are to get in fast, do your work and get out before you are caught in the crossfire.

"There is a plane concealed on a farm to the south of the city. As soon as possible, make for the plane. It will be the only safe way of getting out of the country once the fighting starts."

* * *

The team discussed diversionary tactics over beer and sandwiches. As they were winding up, Gary Warren stuck his head in the door.

"I'm glad I caught you all together. I noticed you had an hour free, so I took the liberty of arranging a screening of our most recent corporate film. The projector's set up in the A/V room down the hall."

As Warren's head disappeared from the door, Ramos snorted. "Less than ten hours to take-off, and all this sniveling little pencil-pusher can think for us to do is watch some stupid movie. How about it, Mama? You want to sneak off somewhere and fool around?"

Mama Dimanche laughed sharply. "Either you have had too much to drink, or your eyesight is not to be trusted." Then she grew grave. When she spoke again, it was in a colder voice that chilled Ramos as he listened. "No. I am very interested in this film. I want to know everything I can about the men behind all this."

* * *

In the end, they all went to watch the film, mostly for want of any better activity. Warren smiled brightly as they took their seats.

"The film you're about to see is entitled 'Islands in the Sun.' It took over a year to make, and I hope it will provide some entertainment as well as information about our operation here."

The lights dimmed and the projector started. The film opened with a rapid intercutting of green forests and blue water, bright lights and showgirls. A suave voice spoke over a driving *salsa* beat.

"Islands in the Sun—just one part of the globe-spanning activities of World Transport Enterprises . . ." The camera zoomed in on a tanned woman in a scant bikini. Ramos whistled and slapped his thigh.

". . . but the Dominican Republic is more than just attractive scenery. It is one of the largest producers of coffee, sugar and spices in the world. Let's look at how WTE has played a part in the development of this island paradise . . ."

Nightshade watched and listened, more intent on what was left unsaid than on what was said. She noted the rapid acquisition of profitable fruit, coffee and sugar markets throughout the Caribbean. Through purchase, merger or distribution, WTE now enjoyed a virtual monopoly on the tropical produce of the Gulf of Mexico.

There was a brief glimpse of Dominican laborers working on the coffee and sugar plantations. Even the clever camera angles and carefully chosen workers could not conceal the lean frames and tired eyes. Then the cameras focused again on the tropical scenery, and the narrator spoke.

"As we continue our search for ways to increase production, and for new markets to conquer, these Islands in the Sun will continue to benefit from the help-ing hand of World Transport Enterprises, the wave of the future . . ." A green wall of water crested and fell, sweep-ing up a golden beach. The Latin rhythm swelled, and the film faded on a bikinied woman walking away from the camera.

As the lights came up, Gary Warren rose, smiling. "Well, I hope this gives you some idea of how you all fit into the big picture here at World Transport. Thanks, and good night." The team rose and returned to the barracks for a few hours of rest.

* * *

Nightshade sat motionless on her cot. The faces of the laborers in the film haunted her. There was a dull lifelessness in their faces, in their movements, that she understood too well. They knew that their destinies were not their own—that forces greater than themselves played with their lives as if they were merely counters in a game. Nightshade understood, because she was one of them.

But, unlike them, she was no longer helpless. She had taken her destiny into her own hands. This 'Carib' opera-tion was very important to the man who controlled World Transport. His hand reached out here to bring thousands more lives under his control. She was closer to her goal now than she had ever been before. Now, while justice was within her grasp, she must be careful, impec-cable. When her opportunity came, she would be ready.

133

19

The rains swept in after midnight. Shortly after two, Carl Ramirez walked past Mama Dimanche's door, knocking loudly.

"Rise and shine, Madame. We meet at the plane in fifteen minutes."

She could hear Ramirez's voice as he woke the others. She sat for a moment, breathing deeply, then was up and gathering her gear. She wrapped a sharp machete in leather and bound it to her calf. She put on a cotton undershirt and two pairs of socks, then pulled on boots and a camouflaged fatigue uniform. A .45 pistol went into a holster, and a knife sat on the other hip. She pulled a beret over the mass of hair, and placed a pair of dark glasses in her shirt pocket. Shouldering her rifle, she sprinted through the rain to the waiting transport.

She helped Martinez work the supply packs into their

parachute harnesses, and double-checked her own pack and chute. She worked her way back into a padded corner of the old plane's fuselage, and rested her head on her pack. The air smelled of gasoline, plastic and wet canvas. The rain drummed relentlessly.

Finally, the last checks were made. Ramirez signalled to the ground and the propellers began to spin. With a bone-jarring roar, the plane started its race down the runway.

* * *

The team tried to make themselves comfortable and rest. The only sounds were the howling winds and the droning of the engine. There was a brief moment of apprehension when a strong headwind caused the props to stall. After a short, heart-twisting dive, the plane righted itself.

Then Carter was pushing his way back past the supplies.

"Ramirez says we're about to break from the cloud cover. We're making our first pass on the drop site. It's a clearing by an old ruined fort. He said to start rigging the supplies. We'll try to jettison them on the next pass."

The packs went out on signal, their black nylon chutes like ebon crosses against the paleness of the clearing below. The engines complained as the plane climbed for a second approach. The door was pushed further open, and the team made fast their cords to the line.

Sharply, the plane banked and dropped below the ragged clouds. The supplies were scattered over several meters of hillside.

As the plane arced in a slow circle, Ramirez's voice shouted the signal, wishing them luck. Ramos jumped. Boyette followed. As Carter bailed out, two chutes blossomed below. Martinez jumped next, and Mama Dimanche threw herself after him, the dragline tripping her chute.

She dropped heavily, the wind whipping at her. Off to her right, Cain was falling. With a jarring jolt, her chute tugged at her armpits, opening wildly. She fought the lines to keep it full.

Suddenly, the ground was racing up to meet her. She braced, hit and rolled, coming up against a canvas sack of watercans. A groan to her right marked Cain's landing. She turned her back to the wind, letting the air straighten the parachute. Quickly rolling it, she tucked it under the water rations and went to find Cain.

He lay on his back, the limp black chute and the billowing green emergency chute hopelessly tangled. She pulled the knife from her belt, cut the shrouds, and the nylon went sailing downhill. Cain, dazed, was rubbing his leg.

"Are you all right?"

"Twisted my ankle," Cain groaned. "Help me up. Let me see if I can walk on it. Oh, Jesus! Christ, that hurts. I better rest here a minute."

Mama Dimanche raised her voice. "Give me a hand over here! Cain's back chute went out. He twisted his leg."

"He'll keep," Boyette's voice boomed back over the wind. "Let's round up the packs while we still can. He can keep an eye on them. Come on!"

Mama Dimanche leaned down to Cain.

"You'll make it?"

"Sure, I'm not going anywhere. Better track down the supplies. We'll need 'em."

* * *

In half an hour, a small pile of olive bundles surrounded Cain. His leg rested on one of them. The rain had turned to light mist, obscuring everything below them. Carter suggested they build a fire and camp until sunrise. Boyette cursed him, and looked at Mama Dimanche.

"This fool wants to advertise our presence to every *marron* and bandit in these hills, and wait for them to come and find us. He will get us killed, eh, Mama?"

She turned to Carter. "Listen, there are only two ways to stay alive up here. One is to kill anything that moves. The other is to keep moving and be invisible, make no sound and cast no shadow. Until we have found the ones we are seeking we must take the second course."

Boyette nodded with satisfaction. Cain had gotten to his feet and was hobbling about, using his rifle as a crutch. His teeth were clenched, but occasionally a gasp would escape them. Boyette came to him with a metal flask.

"Here. Drink this. Let's hope that sprain gets better soon."

"Thanks, Henri." He drank the coarse *clairin* down and coughed. "You don't have to tell me what happens if I can't keep up with you." Cain walked slowly over to the others.

Boyette placed a hand on Mama Dimanche's shoulder. His voice was hot in her ear. "You know these lands better than I, Mama. You must take the lead now, until we have found our *guerrillas*."

To the others, he announced, "Mama Dimanche will be our *corporal* for this leg of the journey. Listen to her, and follow her lead."

"*Merci*. I have two things to say. Do not be too quick with your guns, gentlemen. The *marron*s have all the advantages in this country. And henceforth, you are to speak Creole at all times. If you cannot speak it, be silent. Any questions? *Bon. Allons!*"

Some of the supplies were redistributed to take weight off Cain's injured leg. As they left the ruins of the old fort behind, and began to follow a faint path down the hill, the first gray whispers of dawn lit the low misty clouds to the east.

20

In a secluded grove where a stream widened, a group of men were bathing. Boots, fatigues and weapons were stacked on the bank. A metal can of strong coffee boiled over a small fire. A dozen men splashed or soaked. One man sang, another cursed a third who had stolen his soap.

On the bank, chest bare, a man stood holding a rifle and scanning the surrounding bush. His long wiry hair was touched with gray, and there was a thin seam of an old scar on his shoulder and chest.

He heard a sound. He growled at the men to be silent. Quickly the water-sounds subsided. Somewhere above them on the hillside, something was moving. With a wordless gesture, he motioned the men up on the bank. At his signal, a few stepped into trousers and picked up weapons, and slid into the brush without disturbing the leaves.

They pushed through the foliage, scanning the hillside. Six intruders made slow and arduous progress down the mountain path.

"Who is it, Laval?" whispered one of the men.

The older man noted the shine of the interlopers' boots, and the crispness of their uniforms, and answered, "*Loups garous!*"

They watched as the six continued their descent. When they paused for a moment at a narrow place, Laval raised his hand, then dropped it. Swiftly and silently, the guerrillas attacked.

An arm encircled Martinez's throat. A knife pricked his side. He cried out. Seeing the danger, the team broke for cover. Cain's leg twisted. He pitched forward. A rifle butt struck him down.

Martinez tugged at the strangling arm. Suddenly, a blurred figure struck his assailant. A blow jabbed the guerrilla's arm. It fell limp, the knife dropping to the ground. A jab in the temple knocked him to his knees. As he went black, he saw his attacker's face—a woman's face, with one crimson eye.

The woman struck like a hawk. Men and weapons hit the ground. As she advanced on Laval he whistled sharply, and a dozen more guerrillas burst through the trees.

"Get your hands up, all of you!" Laval commanded.

A dozen guns pointed at the team. Boyette signalled for his men to drop their weapons.

Laval grabbed Carter by his collar. "What have we here?" His eyes flicked over Carter's pale skin. "Who are you? Where do you come from?"

Carter was silent. Laval raised his arm to strike.

"Stop!" cried Boyette in Creole. "We are friends! We seek Ulysse Follette!"

"You and every other stinking wolf and spy the *Président* sends out! Very well, you will have your wish. Tie up these intruders. We will take them back to camp and find out what they are about."

The guerrillas emptied the team's rifles, and bound their arms behind their backs to the rifle stocks. They were lined in single file and prodded through the brush at machete-point.

After several minutes of walking, they came to a small clearing by the stream, where the *marron*s had made camp. Laval called out as they ascended the rise to the campground.

"Ulysse! We have brought you some spies!"

From an old tent made of rotting canvas, a tall ebony man wearing only a black beret and blue jeans stepped forward. He had deep black eyes and a high intelligent brow. He wore a coarse black beard. His shoulders were broad, his arms and hands well muscled.

"What do you want with Ulysse Follette?" His voice was deep and resonant.

"We are exiles," replied Boyette. "We have come across the border to join you, to help you."

"It is a lie, a trick, Ulysse," said Laval. "Look at them, at their fine clothes."

"They do not have the smell of *loups garou*s about them, Claude. What they *are* is another matter."

There was a noise behind them. Laval whirled. Mama Dimanche, unbound, stood upon a log, holding a rifle in her hands.

"How in hell did you get loose? And what can you do with an unloaded gun?"

A bullet whistled past Claude Laval's ear. Half a dozen rifles trained on her.

"Nothing can hold Mama Dimanche—*not even the grave!*"

Laval's mouth gaped open, dumbstruck. He repeated the name under his breath, like an oath. She pointed the rifle at him.

"Now, M'sieur, shall we talk?"

Foulette met her gaze. "Put your gun away, Madame." He nodded to one of his men. "Untie them."

143

The guerrillas slashed the bonds with his knife. Mama Dimanche lowered her rifle, but held it close.

"Now, tell me who you really are, Madame. Mama Dimanche is dead these years past."

"She is who she says, M'sieur Follette," interjected Boyette, "and very much alive as you can see."

Follette sat upon a log. "So, you are Mama Dimanche, risen from the tomb. And these . . . these brave soldiers, they are your men, eh? Why are you here?"

"We wish to help you claim what is yours," replied Boyette, "the trust and support of the people. We wish to aid you in putting an end to the monster who sits in the Presidential Palace."

Boyette gestured to Mama Dimanche. "Mama Dimanche has sworn to take the life of M'sieur *le Président*—alone if she must. But we realize that if no strong leader is at hand to seize power, another such as he may come to rule."

Follette's eyes narrowed as Boyette spoke. Then he laughed. "You think to overthrow the *Président* with a handful of foreigners and a few scruffy *marron*s? A revolution takes time to build, M'sieur."

"You have spent many months in hiding. You underestimate your own popularity. I tell you, the people of Haiti are crying out for a leader to oppose the *Président*. We have brought with us supplies and arms. We wish to go to the capital now, during *Carnaval*, and oppose the bastard's tyranny once and for all!"

"What you say is flattering M'sieur," replied Follette, "but you do not understand our situation here. We are hunted men. The *Président* has sent his troops against us three times this month, and we have barely managed to escape. The peasants are fearful of cooperating with us. Whenever it becomes known that they have aided us there are fierce reprisals. Though the people give us aid and supplies in secret, they would not dare follow us."

"You are wrong, Follette. If you would only go and

ask for help, every able-bodied man among the peasants would join you. You are their only hope. They need your example, your courage to guide them."

"Enough!" said Follette. "We have brought too much tragedy on them already. In the village at the foot of the mountain, a priest was burned alive for cooperating with us. Two daughters of a close friend were raped by the *loups garous* for being too friendly to my men. I will not risk the peasants' lives needlessly!"

Follette drew a deep breath. "A division of *loups garous* is camped near here. Tomorrow or the next day, they will find where we are hiding. Before more tragedy occurs, we must seek safety. In the high mountains south of here there is another guerrilla band. They have resisted the *Président*'s onslaughts for over two years now. We will join them tomorrow. There will be a *combite* in the village tomorrow, and an old friend has promised us provisions for the journey. You are welcome to join us, but I will hear no more of rabble-rousing. I tell you, the time has not come!"

Follette rose as if to go, but Claude Laval stopped him. "Is it wise to discuss our plans with strangers? We do not know who they are!"

"Surely you will accept the word of Mama Dimanche."

Laval turned to the woman. "And how do we know you are she, Madame?"

"Ask any question, set me any test, and I will fulfill it."

A strange smile crossed Laval's face. He glanced at Follette. "Shall I set her such a test, Ulysse?"

"What do you propose?"

"Mama Dimanche was known not only for her skill in battle. She was also known as a powerful *bocur*, a dark witch. Is this not true, Madame?"

She answered only with a look of contempt.

"Then let us have a proof of your skill. I challenge you

to *kanzo*—trial by fire!"

Esteban Ramos turned to Boyette, about to object. Boyette silenced him with a gesture.

There was a silence as the eyes of the men turned to the woman who stood in their midst. When she spoke, fire and ice clashed in her voice.

"Very well. I accept."

* * *

In a sheltered area, Ramos and Boyette spoke together quietly, so as to avoid being overheard.

"This is madness, Henri!" said Ramos. "If I know what she may be forced to undergo, she may be killed. What will this do to our carefully laid plan?"

Boyette smiled. "It is a calculated risk, Esteban . . ."

"A risk? This man would not lead a revolution now if a division of troops crossed the border to support him. How can this mumbo-jumbo help us?"

"If all goes well, I will have this Ulysse Follette in the palm of my hand. And, if our *vodun* witch is a casualty, well, we will survive, Esteban, we will survive."

21

Ulysse Follette had offered the newcomers a share of the *marrons*' meager provisions, despite Laval's objections. Boyette had declined, offering in turn a generous share of their own food. It was the best meal the *marrons* had had in months.

But the meal was disturbed by a tension created by the knowledge of what was to come. As a long-limbed young man left the meal and returned with two small gourd drums, Carter pulled Boyette close.

"What's going on, Boyette? What's gonna happen?"

"*Kanzo* is a *vodun* ritual, Carter, a test of will. It's a trial by fire—walking on coals, or holding a burning branch. If you can bear it without crying out, you've passed the test."

Carter's face twisted. "Do I have to watch?"

Boyette gestured to a man with a gun. "I don't believe we have much choice."

The *marrons* congregated from about the camp, bringing twisted logs and kindling. They built a great pyre over the embers of the campfire. Laval and the drummer placed flat stones on either side of the pyre, and laid a slim log of several feet in length across it. The men formed a great circle about the fire.

As the drummer began a steady rhythm and the sky which deepened overhead began to show points of starlight, flames began to lick at the kindling.

Mama Dimanche stepped into the firelight. The flames cast eerie shadows on her face, causing her crimson eye to gleam demonically. The drumming became more insistent. The men about the fire began to chant an old *vodun* song, and she began to sway with the rhythm, her hips punctuating the steady African beat.

A sinuous snake of yellow flame darted through the bonfire, and twigs crackled and gave sparks to the sky. The voices of the men rose with the flames.

With a great leap, she sprang to the end of the log that spanned the fire. It was beginning to blacken on the bottom, and tongues of flame licked at her bare feet.

Ira Cain strained forward, as if to pull her out.

"Don't go near that fire, Cain!" said Ramos. "The witch got herself into this, now let's see if she can get herself out!"

Suddenly, Mama Dimanche stiffened, contorted, moaned deeply, then cried aloud in an unearthly shriek. She began to tremble all over, a wild expression on her face.

"*Bondieu*!" swore Laval. "She is possessed!"

Few of the men had actually seen a *vodun* possession by the *loa*, where one of the gods took over a human form, but all had heard it described. Now Mama Dimanche's voice crackled out with a vibrancy that seemed to come from all around them.

"*Who calls me?*"

Laval called back in ritual reply, demanding the *loa*'s name.

"*Do you not know me? I am Aida Wedo, Queen of the Loa!*"

The *marron*s stared in mute stupefaction.

Laval spoke again, more softly, his lips trembling.

"O mighty *Aida Wedo*, let this, your servant, prove herself by *kanzo*, by trial by fire!"

"*So be it!*"

The nightmare woman gestured to the fire, and it leapt at her command, causing the men about it to recoil.

As the eyes of all were on the woman in the flames, Henri Boyette left the circle unnoticed, slipping silently into the darkness.

The flames engulfed her. A moment later, the woman called Mama Dimanche sprang from the flames, her garments blazing. Her wild eyes scanned the circle, and seemed to light on something far away. She whirled in a great arc and vanished into the night.

* * *

Boyette moved swiftly through the brush. He must be quick, for soon the *kanzo* ritual would be over, and his presence would be missed. He kept the river on his left, and worked his way down the slope of the moutain. The damp air was still, save for the faint rhythm of the drums, and the newly-risen moon cast a silver sheen over everything.

* * *

Claude Laval stared after the woman who had just emerged, unharmed, like a phoenix, from the flames. He crossed himself, and turned to Follette, whispering, "There can be no doubt, Ulysse. She is Mama Dimanche!"

* * *

Nightshade prowled. The slim, dark figure darted

from tree to tree, as if in pursuit of someone. She would pause a moment, as if listening, then race on.

The flames, the frenzied dancing, the throbbing of the drums, had had an unexpected effect. A dark force had been unleashed on the great mountain. Nightshade was filled with an animal hunger for her prey—an unreasoning, unthinking craving. Until this wild energy, this other possession had spent itself, she could not rest.

She followed the track of scent, sound, swaying branches. Her hands clenched involuntarily. For the first time in many long months, Nightshade was totally in control.

* * *

Boyette turned. Was that a sound? Or were his nerves getting the better of him? Somewhere, a bird took flight, crossing the refulgent moon. Boyette shuddered, and moved more quickly.

* * *

She had lost him. At some point, he had crossed the stream. As she stood in the clearing, under the full moon, the blood-lust began to fade, replaced by an icy calm. She carefully considered her next actions. She could remain here and await his return, or seek him out. She hesitated only a moment, then descended the mountain. When she came to the road, his footprints were fresh in the dry dust.

Suddenly, ahead, she saw him. He was standing near a tar-paper hut that stood by a rough-hewn power pole. He turned, spotting something moving in the moonlight. He flattened against the side of the shack, then broke for the cover of the slopes.

He worked his way back up into the hills. He thought he heard someone following. He stopped by a great twisted tree to await his pursuer, a gun clenched in his fist.

Almost too late, she saw him. His gaze darted to the tree where she stood. She willed herself into immobility, becoming one with the shadows. Boyette advanced a step closer, peering into the darkness. He saw no one. He turned and began to make his way back to the stream.

All the way back to the camp, Boyette felt that someone or some thing dogged his steps. But he could not see it, except out of the corner of his eye, nor hear it distinct from his own steps, his own breath, his own heartbeat. Finally, he heard the sound of drumbeats, signalling that the camp was near, and made for it with careful stealth.

* * *

Nightshade watched from the shadows as Boyette

slipped unseen back into camp. She looked ght. Had she found Boyette while the spirit was upon her, she might have acted recklessly. As it was, he was alert to the presence of something which followed his movements. She would have to be more careful in the future.

What had Boyette been doing? What did he plan? Short of confronting him, there was no way to find out until his actions bore fruit.

As she entered the camp, a sentry passed within a few feet. He saw nothing, and Nightshade slipped into her tent. As she lay on her rough cot, she congratulated herself on the best performance of her life. She wiped the last of the protective ointment from her bare feet. Her eyes closed as the weight of exhaustion finally came down upon her.

22

The *marron* camp slept late. The morning sun had nearly reached its zenith when the first stirrings were heard. Someone blew the smoldering cookfire up to flame and put water on to boil. The smell of warming earth, of ripening mangos and unwashed human beings wove a tapestry of life.

Ramos and Boyette squatted together near the fire, sipping strong coffee.

"So, Henri," said Ramos, "this woman, this Mama Dimanche is everything we expected—and perhaps more than we had bargained for. We asked for an assassin, and we have gotten a she-devil instead. I believe these *marron*s would follow her into the mouth of Hell after last night's show."

Boyette nodded. "There is more, Esteban. While I was out last night, I had the feeling I was being followed. I

155

never got a clear glimpse of whoever it was, but Mama Dimanche disappeared shortly after I left." He shook his head. "You are right, Esteban, she will be of great use to us in the days to come. However, when she has served her purpose . . ."

"She must be killed. She is too dangerous to be allowed to live."

Boyette agreed, sorry though he was to see such an interesting woman die.

* * *

The *marron*s were wary of the witch woman when she came to share their meal, viewing her with mingled fear and awe. Ulysse Follette came to sit beside her.

"I sought you last night, Madame, to say these words. I will say them now. At first I doubted you, even as my men did. After last night, there can be no doubt. I would be proud to have you and your men march beside us."

"Thank you, Ulysse." There was a strange coolness in her voice. "I hope I shall not give you cause to regret your decision." She rose quickly. Follette watched her go, shrugged, and went to ready his men for the long march.

* * *

By noon, camp was broken. There was little left of the encampment save rutted earth and the remnants of the fires. The guerrilla band massed to listen to their leader.

"We will follow the road to the farm where the *combite* is to be held. Marcel Degous has promised us supplies and provisions for our journey. You are to make Mama Dimanche and her men welcome among you. We should reach Debec's camp by nightfall. *En avant, mes amis!*"

He shouldered his pack, and they set out in a long, ragged line down the mountain.

* * *

The band traveled for some time down the twisty mountain path, coming to a small footbridge where they dipped their canteens in the fresh water. Beyond the bridge, the path joined the road.

As Follette and Mama Dimanche walked down the dusty road, a strange wailing-horn call floated through the air, followed by an insistent drum rhythm. Mama Dimanche looked up quickly.

"Surely you have not been away so long that the call to a *combite* startles you?"

The woman smiled faintly. "No. My surprise was one of pleasure. I had thought I would not live to hear one again."

23

As the road passed a peasant village, it forked. One branch continued straight, showing rutted tire tracks; the other was a winding footpath, veering up into the hills. They turned up the ragged trail.

The undergrowth thickened and flies troubled the men as the road grew steeper. Once more the conch-shell horn sounded the *combite*.

They could hear the sound of singing and the steady beat of the drummers. As they crested the hill, they saw below rows of men, half naked, sweating in the sun as their hoes swung in unison to the rhythm of the drummer. There was much laughter, and snatches of song rose to the listeners. One song seemed to refer to a bit of village gossip, and the singers repeated each line with relish.

Follette gestured proudly, as he spoke "This is the *combite*, the heart of Haitian Communism. The men of the village come to work for an afternoon on one man's field. They are paid only by a small feast at the end of the day. Tomorrow, they will work on another field, for another man. So, the land of every villager is prepared for the sowing in half the time it would take for each to do it alone. Everyone gets his crop in, and the whole village eats for another year. More, the work is joyous, full of laughter and singing, because a man is working beside his fellows. I will make a *combite* of the whole of Haiti, and our land will prosper. This is my inspiration, my dream."

Work stopped as the workers saw the *marrons* making their way down from the hill. Follette shouted to draw the men near, and gestured for Mama Dimanche to stand beside him.

Two men left the workers to join them. One was tall, heavy and lined, with graying hair. The other was young, perhaps nineteen or twenty.

"Ulysse!" cried the older man. "What brings you from the hills, today of all days? The *loups garous* are scouring the countryside looking for your men. You must—"

He stopped suddenly, lifting the crucifix about his neck as if warding the evil eye.

Follette laughed. "Do not be afraid, Marcel. Surely you have heard of Mama Dimanche. She has just returned from across the border with able men to aid our cause."

Mama Dimanche bowed. Degous relaxed visibly.

"We cannot stay long, Marcel. We have come to purchase provisions for a long march southward. We have brought much tragedy upon you. We must go before more harm is done."

"You know you are always welcome here, Ulysse," said Degous. He put his arm around the young man with him. "This young man is Roger Fournier, Ulysse. It is his day today; we work to prepare his field for planting."

Follette clasped Roger's hand firmly. An admiring

look danced in Roger's eyes.

Degous looked up, shading his eyes. "I see that you come to us with much to discuss. It is nearly time for the mid-afternoon rest. Since the work goes well, we will call a halt and give these tired men of yours a bit of food and drink, eh, Roger?"

Roger agreed, and went to call the men to the great canvas awning under which were spread simple foods and cool earthen pitchers of drink.

The *marron*s crouched or sat on the ground, some dipping water from a great kettle, others stripping off shirts and tying them about their waists. A group of men equal in number soon came from the fields, panting from their exertions. A few hailed the *marron*s by name, but many viewed them with a mixture of interest and suspicion. Roger circulated quietly, bidding the men to make them welcome. As an example, he broke a piece of bread and gave it to Follette. Follette thanked him, praising highly Roger's new wife, who had baked it.

The people seemed to relax at the ritual gesture of good will. Boyette and Cain mingled with the workers, drinking wine and joking.

Mama Dimanche excused herself to walk among the women of the village. At first they deferred to her as if she were one of the soldiers, but soon they had overcome their awe, and were eager to talk with her.

The women spoke of the same things: children, the crops, how hard it was to make a profit at market since the *loups garous* came. Under the idle talk was a stubborn, lean optimism in spite of the hardships of life, which left Mama Dimanche with a new respect for them.

Thanking them for their hospitality, she excused herself and returned to the shelter. She found Ramos and Boyette in close conference. As she drew near, she heard Boyette speak in a low tone.

"Such a picture of idyllic peace, Esteban. A pity it will not last until sunset."

161

She stepped forward. Boyette looked up quickly.

"Ah, Madame. We were just—"

There was a sharp report like gunfire.

Mama Dimanche whirled. The sound of car motors whining up a grade was heard. As she peered at the top of the hill, into the sun, a pair of aging jeeps, painted black, crested the grade.

Women screamed. Children fled to their mothers. The men set down their food and drink. Follette's rifle came up.

As the jeeps drew closer, she could see that each held two men in black shirts with white berets and belts. All wore oversized dark glasses, and held guns at ready.

Follette swore softly.

"It is the *loups garous*!"

The jeeps drove across a field, heedless of the tilled earth, and swung quickly to a halt before the pavillion. A great, fat man got out slowly from the passenger seat of the forward jeep, his weapon held lax in his hand, a broad white smile on his fleshy face. Three *loups garous*, younger and leaner, ranged behind him, their guns cocked. He strolled forward, past motionless peasants, to where Follette and Degous stood. He carelessly dipped his hand in a bowl of fruit, selecting a ripe piece.

He stood, regarding Follette, seeming heedless of the guerrilla's gun, and ate the fruit in a few great bites. Finally he spoke, in a thick, heavy voice.

"Nice of you to throw us a party, Marcel. The boys were getting hungry." He regarded Follette. "And what is this? It stinks like a mountain goat, but walks on its hind legs! No, I am wrong. It is the bastard, Follette!"

A deep laugh began, and was cut off by a smashing backhand blow by Follette. The fat *loup garou* staggered back, and three rifles prepared to cut Follette down.

The *loup garou* restrained his men with a whisper.

"Not yet boys. We want to take him alive."

He walked past them, his henchmen watching warily

for a sign of violence. He raised his hands high above his head, bellowing out in a great booming voice.

"Hear me! Listen well, all of you. I have warned all of you before, as I warned your new priest—*I* am the head man in these parts. My word is law! I told you all that any man found helping these mountain bandits would pay with his life. However . . ." He paused to observe the effects of his words. The peasants were stricken with fear.

"However, I will make a bargain with M'sieur Follette. He comes along with me, peaceful-like and gentle, and nobody gets hurt. What do you say to that, eh, Follette?"

The *marrons* looked anxiously at their leader. He breathed deeply and took a pace forward.

"Very well. It is a bargain. I am yours."

A chilling voice cut him off. "NO! It must not be!"

The great hulking *loup garou* turned to the interruption, his submachine gun ready. "Who speaks?"

From between the ranks of *marrons*, a nightmare apparition strode forward. Mama Dimanche, her one eye gleaming wildly, a sharpened machete raised in challenge to the chieftain, walked boldly to within inches of the gunbarrel.

"I speak. I am Mama Dimanche!"

Terror clouded the arrogant visage of the *loup garou*. He raised his weapon with trembling hands, speaking only half-coherently.

"But—but that's impossible! Mama Dimanche is dead, slain—you can't be!"

The woman tossed her head in defiance. When she spoke, there was a pervasive quality to her words which seemed to come from all directions. "The *loa* would not let me die. I live to wage war on pigs like you, and to capture the head of the *Président!*" She began to weave the glinting blade of her machete about, and the chief stood stupefied, watching the serpentine motions like a small animal bewitched by a snake. As the blade neared his face, he shook his head vigorously, shaking off the spell.

"We will see if you cannot die, witch!"

He threw the gun bolt forward to fire, and his three henchmen moved in unison to cover him. Before he could fire, a swift striking blow from Dimanche's free hand sent the machine gun flying from his hands. He dove for it, but her boot kicked it out of reach toward the *marron*s. With a bellow of rage, he threw himself at Mama Dimanche. She staggered backwards before the assault, gripping his arm, and ducking under and up to pin it behind him. The machete came up under his double chins and pressed tenderly.

The *loups garous* froze.

"Do not move, Mama Dimanche commands it—or else, the *loa* will have a new pig for the sacrifice!" The henchmen swung their guns to her head, and the chief sputtered, "You fools! Be careful! You could kill me!"

There was a palpable tension in the air as the seconds ticked by. The *loup garou* chief had ceased to struggle actively, his fearful eyes darting back and forth looking for hope. A few of the *marron*s began a slow advance on the guards. Slowly, they began to back toward the jeeps.

"Cowards!" cried the chief. "Where are you going?"

Unnoticed, Boyette slowly raised his pistol and fired a single shot.

One of the *loups garous* dove behind the jeep, recklessly spraying bullets. A young peasant fell to the earth, bleeding. Most of the rest ran for shelter. Follette and the *marron*s took cover behind tables and brush. Mama Dimanche and her terrified captive stood alone together in the clearing.

One by one, the *marron*s, led by Follette, began to advance on the remaining henchmen, firing their handguns. The *loups garou*s fell back, laying down a heavy barrage of fire. Two *marron*s fell, and a peasant who vaulted over the jeep with a machete was cut down.

Boyette and Ramos, as if one, detached themselves

from the crossfire, and began to circle slowly in great arcs up the side of the hill, ducking behind clumps of brush. One of the *loups garous* wheeled about, covering the others' flank.

Mama Dimanche shouted over the chaos that she would slit the throat of the chief if the men did not cease fire. There was only a slight pause, and the guns began again. The chief began to curse his own men for their treachery.

He broke Mama Dimanche's grip in a fit of fear and desperation. They struggled over the machete. His great mass began to force the blade close to the woman's face. It bit, leaving a thin red line, then was forced back. They hung, poised, limbs trembling.

Then the chief gasped, choking. Follette's rifle had cut him down. He slumped slowly to the ground.

* * *

Almost as quickly as the battle had begun, it was over. Boyette's handgun drilled through the skull of one of the *loups garous*. The others were shot by the *marrons* as they attempted to flee.

Ten men lay dead. The *loup garou* chieftain lay on his back, eyes open, a red stain spreading across his chest. His three henchmen were contorted in grotesque postures. One was slumped over the steering wheel. Two peasants were dead, and Follette had lost four of his men, including Claude Laval, felled by a single bullet in the back. A half dozen more were wounded.

The silence following the battle finally brought the peasants from shelter. They stared in open-mouthed awe at the spectacle of bloodshed. One young woman, seeing her slain lover lying motionless, attempted to raise his head. It fell heavily, and she rent the air with lamentation, crooning over him. The peasants kept clear of the *loups garous*, as if suspecting that some dark sorcery would reanimate them again. In most of their faces was a dull terror of the inevitable retribution this would bring.

A few of the young men, led by Roger, had a different look, as if the awareness of their new power had just dawned on them. Had they not slain the *loups garou*s who were supposed to be protected by the charms of the *Président* himself? What more could they dare?

Henri Boyette took Roger Fournier's arm. He spoke quickly in a low, electric voice.

"You have done it, Roger! You have thrown off the shackles of the *Président*'s troops." He whispered in a confidential tone. "Listen. Follette plans to march south from here to join another guerrilla band. With the aid of the famous *mambo* Mama Dimanche, he could even take the capital! But our numbers are small. We have need of strong, dedicated men like yourself."

Boyette waited while his words took effect, then continued, "These people respect you, Roger. What would they think of you if you did not join Follette now when the day is ripe for it?" Seeing the hesitation in the young man's face, he spoke more urgently. "Soon, word of this will reach the *Président*'s men. There is little time. Go now, speak to your friends, Roger."

As Boyette saw the flame of battle kindle in the young man's eyes, a smile touched his lips.

Follette came to Mama Dimanche, who stood with the hot wind disturbing her hair, and a trickle of blood lining her face. Her eyes barely saw the bodies. He put a hand on her shoulder, giving her a rough cloth to stanch the flow of blood.

She spoke as if from a great distance.

"So it begins, eh, Ulysse? The slaughter, the killing. So soon . . ."

Follette regarded her with a look of surprise. "Surely this is what you and your men had in mind, Mama. Can it be your long years of exile have softened you to the harsh realities of warfare? Are you indeed the same woman who fought with the *Président*'s men and neither gave nor expected mercy these years past?" He rolled the *loup garou* chief over with his outstretched boot. "Indeed it begins, Mama. And once begun, it cannot be halted."

Mama Dimanche looked up to see two figures approaching.

"It is Marcel and Roger. You know you are a hero to them now, Ulysse."

"If you had not acted as you did, I might have been a dead hero, Mama. For this, I thank you." Mama Dimanche was silent.

As Marcel Degous approached, he clasped Follette's hand firmly.

"We owe you a debt, Ulysse. Without you, your men, we could not have stood up to these pigs. Now they will trouble us no more."

"I fear your troubles have only begun. Where the *Président*'s men are concerned, we are all outlaws now. Your kin have fought bravely," his voice faltered, "and paid dearly. Our coming has brought ill fortune on you, my friend. We must go before we cause more tragedy."

Young Roger spoke. "No, Ulysse. The time had come. Were we to spend the rest of our lives at the mercy of *cocoyens* such as these? No, we must fight. If you go to the capital to strike a blow against the *Président*, I for one will go with you."

Boyette raised his gun to the sky, shouting, "*Vive Follette! Vive la Revolution!*"

The peasants took up the chant. The air shook with their cries. Boyette turned to Ulysse Follette.

"These people are crying for a champion, a leader, Follette. You cannot refuse them!"

Follette's chin lifted. A fire danced in his eyes.

"Too long have we lived in these hills, hunted and chased like rabbits . . ." His face hardened. "If it is the will of the people, I must follow it."

Boyette smiled fiercely in triumph. The trap was

sprung. The plan had worked to perfection. Now he need only let events take their course.

Marcel spoke softly. "Roger, you are newly wed. You have a big farm, and may yet have many children. Let the men without families go with Follette. Your place is here."

"No, Uncle. Now that we have finally acted, no place will be safe for us. We must finish what we have started." Roger looked about at the young men of the village. "How many of you are with me? Follette goes to the capital to put an end to the bastard once and for all. I am going with him. Let those of you who love freedom speak now!"

Several young men stepped forward, declaring themselves for Follette. Many more spoke their fears and regrets frankly, saying there was too much at stake. Roger, a fire in his eyes, would have condemned them for cowards, had not Follette interceded.

"I understand those of you who cannot go with us. The lot of a guerrilla is a hard one. One fills one's belly with freedom and hope in place of food. I do not hold any of you to a pledge. Let those who are willing, come with us now. For the rest, *grace al' Bondieu.*"

* * *

Follette made his farewells as the afternoon shadows lengthened, and the soldiers readied their gear for the march ahead. At the insistence of Mama Dimanche, Roger and two other men were provided with handguns.

Roger kissed his young wife goodbye, her eyes glistening with tears. Doubled in size, the fledgling army set to find the camp of the guerrillas in the south.

24

As the rebels took to the road, Boyette sent Cain and Martinez among them to encourage them in their revolutionary fervor. He had learned from years of such work that these times of high hopes and spirits were the best times to influence the minds of the impressionable. He himself fell in step with young Roger, who marched behind Follette, and through a combination of flattery and praise for Follette attempted to win over the young peasant.

Carter was dispatched down the line to hand out money and food. Martinez had chided Carter for disappearing from sight during the battle. The American had shrugged, saying simply that it was not his fight.

Mama Dimanche seemed withdrawn, and often went ahead to see that no one lay in wait for the loud and ragged group. As they continued the march, laden with supplies which would be vital in the mountain crossing of the following day, she saw that the newcomers broke into two groups. Some, like Roger, were full of the spirit of revolution, and though inexperienced would make dedicated fighters. But nearly half had come for some other reason, whether by virtue of the spoils they hoped to take, or merely shame at being left behind. These were restive under their burdens, often wanting to call a halt for the slightest pretext.

As night fell, and the band began the climb into the foothills where Debec's bandits and marauders were encamped, Follette split his *marrons* into a front and rear guard surrounding the peasants. Finally, as they crossed a stream, Follette bade the group to wait on the other side, and he and a small band went ahead. Boyette insisted on going with him, and Mama Dimanche did also. Follette shrugged, leaving the combined group in the care of Ramos and Cain.

Almost immediately they were challenged by a ragged young man with an old gun.

"Who are you?"

"I am Ulysse Follette. Where is Debec?"

"Follette? It is you, eh? And who are these strange ones with you?"

Follette quickly named Mama Dimanche. The young rebel crossed himself, and nodded as Follette pointed out the rest. The sentry gestured ahead of him with his gun.

"Go ahead, but carefully. There are others waiting armed like me. I will lead you to Debec."

* * *

Follette was welcomed warmly by Debec and his men, though he cast a cool glance at the others. Unlike Follette's well-trained, hardened group, this band seemed little more than fugitives. They were ill supplied and had few arms. The men were emaciated and their clothing hung in rags, barely covering them. There was not a shoe among them. Their faces were lined, and many bore scars telling of battle or imprisonment.

Debec taunted Follette a little, though in a good-natured manner. Mama Dimanche gathered there was an old hostility between their families over political matters. It seemed somehow meaningless in their squalor. Debec also was somewhat in awe of Mama Dimanche.

After a hard private palaver between the two guerilla leaders, Debec, speaking for his ragged band of little more than a dozen, agreed to go with Follette. Two things seemed to convince him. One was the obvious affluence of Boyette, and the promise of good food and arms which Follette's new patrons seemed to bring.

The other reason seemed to be a fear that when the deaths of the *loups garous* were discovered, reinforcements would scour the hills in search of them. Safety lay in numbers. Debec was unwilling to leave the hills on short notice, and offered to clear his campsite to make room for the newcomers. Mama Dimanche noted that the desperate life of a hill bandit had sharpened his sense of strategy. He was eager to discuss their brave and reckless scheme.

The rest of the rebels were escorted across the river by Debec's men, and the laborious business of making camp for the night began. It grew late as Boyette and his men began to dish out food drawn from the combined stores of the three factions. Debec's men eyed the bowls of stew with ravenous hunger, some devouring three or four helpings.

Boyette considered quietly the problem of getting enough food to feed the growing army. For tonight he must let it pass in order to gain the good will of these cagy but hungry fighters. A more serious problem had presented itself as a small group talked tactics by the fire. Debec, Follette, Mama Dimanche and Boyette and his men sat outside the tents in a close circle.

"But there is still the problem of arms and uniforms, Ulysse," Debec was saying. "My men at least ought to have good footgear and a rifle and ammunition each. Perhaps these farmers should be given guns, too, if they can figure out how to use them."

Boyette spoke up, across the fire from Debec.

"We anticipated such a problem, M'sieur. We have a plan to remedy it."

"What is this plan?"

"The Hinche garrison has arms and supplies enough for ten times our strength. Take the garrison, and they are ours."

"They outnumber us ten to one," Follette responded sharply. "Besides, they are trained soldiers. It would be a massacre."

"Not necessarily. My friend and comrade, Señor Martinez has brought something which should be very effective. Manuel?"

Martinez smiled, his teeth gleaming. He pulled from his bag a small plastic case. He opened it to display a series of small glass cylinders filled with a blue liquid.

"With this, there will be no resistance."

"Poison," Debec barely whispered.

Martinez nodded.

"Enough to kill every man, woman and child within a hundred mile radius of here. One of these would be enough to disable the garrison."

Debec's face tensed, as if thinking.

"Most of the soldiers are camped in the garrison. Their water comes from a single well in the middle of the camp. In order to stop also the officers who stay with their families, we would have to plant some in the great well in the town square. . ."

"No! I will not have innocent lives taken!" Follette was on his feet.

"But Ulysse," Debec said appeasingly, "we cannot afford to take the chance. If the officers interrupt our raid, we might lose our lives—before we ever got a chance to take the capital."

But Follette was adamant. His gaze swung about the campfire, resting at last on Mama Dimanche.

"Mama, surely you will not endorse so brutal a tactic simply to provide us with boots. If you do this, you go alone!"

Mama Dimanche answered quickly. "We must take our chances with the one well in the garrison. It is some distance from the village, and less traffic passes through. If the work is done before the evening meal we can be in and away by nightfall and none will know for hours. Besides. . ." Here she turned to Boyette. ". . .we need Follette's support, eh Henri? It is essential to our plan, is it not?"

Boyette's lips tensed, as if suppressing hostility. Then he quietly agreed. "Yes, There is wisdom in these suggestions. But we must be swift when we make the raid. I myself will plant the poison. Señor Martinez or any of you would be too conspicuous. And one more thing. Nothing is to be said to the peasants. If they ask how it happens that there is no resistance, we will tell them it is a powerful spell by the *mambo bocur*—a deep sleep."

"Very well," said Follette, "we will march to the woods outside Hinche tomorrow, and remain there until your work is done. Then we will march in swiftly and arm these men." He stepped from the fire. "It grows late. Let us rest for the coming day. We have much to do tomorrow."

* * *

The peasants had made camp near the cookfires. Now the night grew chill, and the men wrapped themselves in blankets. The fires died down, and soon the camp was asleep.

Boyette realized that Dimanche and Follette were

away somewhere, but was irritated enough by the mysterious woman not to go looking for her. He called together the team and assigned each of them to a shift on watch. They were to patrol the perimeter of the camp and make sure that no one left the area. Boyette himself drew the first shift. The rest turned in for some sleep.

Follette and Mama Dimanche, in her tent, spoke long into the night. She was trying to understand the guerilla and his life, without betraying herself.

Follette's father had been an official under the rule of the old *Président* but had brought the wrath of the secret police down upon him by defending the poor against the incessant demands of the Bureau of Contributions. He was accused of being a Marxist, and a warrant of death was put on the entire family.

Ulysse was sent to Paris, but his father and mother were not so fortunate. It was said that his mother was shot, trying to escape the advances of the *loups garous*. Rumor had it that his father was tortured to death by the *Président* himself, a dubious honor. Follette didn't know how or when his parents actually died.

He completed his education in Paris, supported by friends of his family. When he was twenty-five he decided to return to Haiti. His studies of history and politics inflamed him with the dream of establishing a purely communistic government of the people in his homeland.

Follette was not a supporter of Russia, or of China. He felt that those giants had strayed from the true path. Under him Haiti was to be no puppet, but through group effort would raise itself out of the morass of poverty. He was, he said, an admirer of Ho Chi Minh, who followed his own path.

He spoke of the people of Haiti, how poor they were, how hungry. Mama Dimanche asked what Follette intended to do about the *loups garous*, the secret police of the *Président*'s regime. At this Follette became angry.

"Those scum! The people themselves will see to it.

176

When the poor know that they need not fear government reprisal, the werewolves will vanish forever into the night they came out of. No, they are the only citizens of this island that I have no pity for."

"I hope that what you wish can come to pass," she replied. "There is much evil on this island, and it should be laid to rest. I believe you are an honest man, Follette, and I will be proud to help you gain power." She rose, and walked to the door of the tent. "I pray you will stay there." With those words she was gone.

Follette looked after her curiously. It seemed to him that Mama Dimanche should have known his history. Perhaps she was only testing him, as he had tested her. He rolled himself in his blankets, then fell asleep.

* * *

Boyette walked the perimeter of the camp. Checking his watch, he noted that it was nearly time to wake Carter for the second shift. He stopped to rest, his eyes carefully, slowly, scrutinizing the darkness to his right, to his left, then quickly they fixed upon a shadow. It moved again. He eased silently toward the man in the brush.

A painfully gaunt man of about thirty was trying to leave the camp without noise. He looked behind him repeatedly. Boyette recognized him as one of the peasants who had expressed doubts about the attempt at revolution. Boyette fingered at something in his pocket. The man was moving toward him, and would have to be induced to turn around. When the man was within about four feet of him, Boyette tossed a small rock. The clatter made the man whirl to see what was behind him. The moment his back was turned, Boyette leapt out and tossed a garrotte around the man's neck and brought him to his knees.

"Where do you think you're going?" Boyette demanded.

"To the bushes," the shocked man croaked, "to the bushes, I swear it."

"I don't think so. You were too worried about being followed. You were going to find a friendly soldier, weren't you?"

"Please don't kill me. . .I'll tell you."

"Oh, I won't kill you, my friend. Just tell me where you were going." Boyette loosened the wire a little so the man could speak.

"There are *loups garous* about a mile from here. I hoped for a little reward. They will catch us anyway. Better to save my life, and make a little money, too."

Boyette grunted, and swiftly tightened the garrotte. In a moment the man was dead. He looked at the corpse. He went through the pockets, and pulled out a few gourdes.

"A pity, now you have no money . . . and no life either." Boyette dragged the body into the bush, and covered it with loose leaves. He was far enough from the camp that he was sure no one would find it.

Boyette wiped his hands on his trousers, then headed back to camp to wake Carter. His turn at watch was over.

Ten yards away, another shadow moved. Nightshade drew closer to the still form, brushing away a few leaves. She stared down at the dead man for several moments, then covered him up again. It was too late to do anything for him.

But perhaps it was not too late to have some effect on the outcome of this grisly adventure. She had infiltrated determined to find some way to sabotage the plans of World Transport and the mysterious figure who stood behind it. Her personal vendetta had blinded her to the fate of these, the other victims of his expediency.

How could she continue to be a party to this, even if her subsequent actions did injure the man she sought? If she did not commit the assassination, the carefully laid

plan would go astray, but the people of this land would
continue to suffer under the iron heel of the *Président*.
But if she did fulfill her mission, then a new tyrant would
come to rule these people, and leave them even poorer as
the fruits of the land were stolen by World Transport.

A grim smile twisted her lips. If only there were some
way this crazy revolution could actually succeed, some
miscalculation or error on someone's part. With Follette
in the palace, at least the people would be assured of a
leader who would listen to their problems and care more
about human needs than about politics.

Nightshade toyed with the idea for a moment,
fascinated. Then she shook her head. It was not the time.
Follette and his men must have a strong, well armed
force behind them to succeed. If fate should give her the
opportunity, she would seize it. For now, she must con-

tinue to play this charade a little longer. She slipped silently back to her tent, easily avoiding the eyes of Carter, now on sentry duty.

25

Camp was struck quickly after the morning meal. The peasants, who had slept badly in the rude surroundings, were quarrelsome, and Cain was given the task of appeasing them with encouragement and tobacco. A tenuous camaraderie was struck as one of Debec's men began a bawdy Haitian folk tune. Although he improvised the verses as they marched, often making obscene digs at the *Président* and his men, all of the line joined in on the choruses as they made their way down the hills. They seemed less soldiers that morning than a group of overgrown boy scouts off on a hike.

Ramos wanted to regiment them into files and ranks, and was nervous about the booming sound of their voices, but Mama Dimanche overruled him, stressing the need for *esprit de corps*. Ramos grumbled, insisting that they assume a more military appearance when they reached level ground.

The descent was complete before noontime. The marching was easier now, in the level and fertile valley of the *Rivière Guayamouc*, and the small army quickly cover the seven miles to the *Thomassique* road. Here there was danger of discovery as well as observation from planes overhead in the restricted airspace. Follette called a halt, urging the men to march quickly and in an orderly manner to the camping area outside Hinche.

They crossed the road unseen. They followed a dirt track through the countryside, and would occasionally pass a child or an old woman with a basket on her head. The peasants would leave the road in fear and give them passage, believing that it was a division of the *Président*'s men who trekked through the fields. Finally, in a small grove by a secluded bend in the river, four kilometers east of Hinche, they made their camp, resting by the water.

Here, Mama Dimanche made another attempt to gain some control over the plan to poison the garrison, insisting that she be allowed to go in with Boyette. To her surprise, it was Follette who offered an objection.

"I am afraid M'sieur Boyette is correct, Mama. You are a striking woman. Even garbed as a peasant you would be too noticeable. It is best that Boyette move swiftly in and out, alone."

She was unable to argue, for to do so would have been to suggest that she herself did not trust Boyette. She kept her peace. Shortly after, Boyette, dressed in a white ragged peasant shift, slipped out of camp toward the garrison at Hinche.

Boyette had strapped the vials of poison to his waist, and concealed a handgun in the loose folds of his clothing. Now he approached the settlement openly, head bowed. He stooped by the shoulder of the road to rub some dirt under his fingernails, and proceeded on. There was no time to waste, for the women would begin dinner preparations in less than an hour.

A mangy dog snarled at him as he entered the outskirts

of the village. To his left rose the great walls of the garrison. An indolent young soldier lounged near the sentry box in the afternoon heat, drinking a bottle of *clairin*. Boyette walked slowly past the soldier who barely noticed him as he entered the compound. The peasants came and went here in the center square of the garrison, often setting up stalls for the soldiers on market days.

He walked forward toward the stone well. He wiped his forehead with the sleeve of his shirt, as if overheated, then reached for the old metal ladle which hung by the well. He dipped it in and took a long drink, peering cautiously over the rim. Lowering the half-empty dipper, he quickly emptied a vial of poison into it, then dropped the undrunk water back into the well, replacing the ladle.

He walked quickly, but without undue haste away from the well, smiling insipidly at the guard at the gate. Boyette turned the corner and was away, unnoticed. He paused at the crossroads outside the garrison. He would not have enough time to reach the main settlement at Hinche before the cooking began, but there was, so Debec said, a cluster of houses with a small cistern just off the main road, where many of the officers had their homes.

When he determined that no one could see him, he went sprinting with long strides down the road. In a few minutes he had come upon a group of whitewashed houses with neat gardens and bright metal roofs. He walked languidly up to the cistern, filling it with the toxin as he had the one in the military camp, and was gone.

He left the settlement the way he had come, moving swiftly as the shadows lengthened. Back at the encampment by the river, he found the camp at rest. He found a shady spot and settled down for a peaceful nap.

* * *

Boyette woke promptly at sunset, and went to rouse

183

the rest of his team.

"Time to go. Get everybody up. We've got four kilometers to cover before nightfall."

The ragged army pulled itself together, and set out. This time they took the road.

As they approached Hinche in the gathering twilight, even Ramos was struck by the eeriness of the scene. The once bustling town was silent. There were a few crumpled bodies on the street, but no other signs of human beings. A few cooking fires smouldered, the tree branches stirred in the breeze, but that was the only movement. The silence infected the rebel army, and they moved like ghosts through the streets.

The front guard approached the armory, and halted. Tattered rows of peasants formed close behind them. Follette and Mama Dimanche went in first. All was silent. There were a few guards lying dead in the corridors, nothing more. Outside, Cain cautioned the peasants not to drink from the well.

After scouting for survivors, and finding none, Follette and Dimanche returned and signalled that all was clear. The troup entered, and Ramos began passing out guns and knives. Martinez went in to scout for explosives for the assault on Port-au-Prince. Boyette suggested that those without foot gear should find boots. Under Ramos's urging the men looked through the dead soldiers until they found clothes and shoes to fit.

In an hour it was done. Where a ragged band of peasants had entered Hinche, an army marched out. Each was was well clothed, carried a pack loaded with food and weapons. Martinez loaded his pack with demolition equipment and explosives. Ramos was pleased at his new army. Here was a real threat, worthy of Dominican military intervention.

But for all their military finery, the spirit which had carried them through the morning was shattered by the sight of the slain. As they trudged south through the deepening twilight, Mama Dimanche saw a young child lying limply on the ground beside a cloth doll. For a moment she hoped the child slept, but she knew that Boyette had taken no chances. She considered calling it to Follette's attention, then gave up, seeing the futility of the gesture. Again the hand of expediency had reached out and taken innocent lives. Nightshade marched beside the peasants, a cold fury raging inside of her.

It was a forced march. There was a pall of silence on the rebel band. Follette hoped to get at least to the outskirts of Bouli, putting both distance and the rough and unpaved path through the mountains between them and pursuing forces. He had to keep driving the rebels onward, for their own safety.

At last they came upon the mountain trail, barely visible in the near darkness. The going was rough, the trail overgrown. Mama Dimanche was glad at least that the peasants had boots. They had to make good time to get out of the Hinche reserve before daybreak when the first hints of trouble might reach the capital.

Shortly after midnight the rebel army made its way through a pass, and out of the restricted area around Hinche. A mile or so outside of Bouli, Follette ordered a halt. The men were exhausted, and many were still numb from the death at Hinche. The few who had entertained thoughts of betrayal dismissed them now. If the witch-woman could do that to over a thousand soldiers, what hope did a single traitor have?

They made camp near a small stream. Tents were pitched, hidden by branches and leaves. The men ate, drank water, then slept.

In a large tent, well away from the others, Ramos and Boyette unpacked a small, powerful radio transmitter. Aiming the antenna toward the Dominican Republic, Ramos sent an identification signal to Ramirez, still at the base they had left only three nights before. When the answering pulse came, Ramos spoke quietly, in Spanish.

"This is 'Carib.' We have completed Sections One and Two, over."

"Acknowledge. Sections One and Two complete. Proceed as scheduled. Maintain radio silence until 24 hours from goal, over and out."

Ramos swiftly shut down the radio set as soon as the message had been received. The government's electronic ears were always scanning the island. A transmission that short left no time to take a fix.

Ramos nodded with satisfaction.

"It goes well, Henri. General Cruz will mobilize as soon as Ramirez gives him the signal. In two days time we should be within striking distance of the capital."

* * *

Alone in her tent, the woman called Nightshade lay in darkness. The faces of the slain hung before her eyes. She was sickened by the wholesale slaughter, and her heart went out to this poor, hungry, terrorized land. As she slipped at last into sleep, she was troubled by old nightmares—memories of pain and flames, the horror she had tried to banish through vengeance.

26

The sparkling South African Airlines charter jet-liner whined up to the gate at Miami International Airport. The mobile corridor nosed out, and gently kissed the side of the plane. An attractive flight attendant opened the door, then returned to the cabin.

"We've landed, gentlemen. You may disembark now." She smiled, and went forward to speak to the captain.

Four burly men in their mid-twenties, all blond and blue-eyed, moved to the door. They were dressed in identical European tailored white suits, and dark ties emblazoned with stylized globes.

They were followed by a tall, graying man, also dressed in white. His features were regular and tanned, with a patrician nose and deep blue eyes. He was a distinguished looking man who carried himself with a military air, and flourished a silver walking stick.

Four more bodyguards fell in behind. The nine men were the only passengers aboard that huge aircraft.

Passing through the corridor, the men emerged into a luxurious passenger lounge. Thick carpets covered the floor. There were a few chrome and leather chairs in intimate groupings, and the lighting was subtle. The luggage from the plane was stacked in one corner near a long counter from behind which two men stepped out. They introduced themselves as U.S. Customs and Immigration officers, and apologized for the necessary delay.

"No need to apologize, gentlemen. I understand the necessary formalities." The tall, distinguished man spoke softly, with a cultivated British accent.

"Ah—yes, sir." The Immigrations official seemed embarrassed. "If I could have your passports, please."

Nine passports bearing the seal of the Republic of South Africa were handed to him. He flipped through them quickly, checking the visas, stamped them with the entry date, initialed them, and courteously handed each back to its owner.

The Customs official spoke up. "Would you please bring the luggage over here?"

The regal South African looked at two of the men, and they quickly brought the suitcases over and placed them on the counter.

"Have you anything to declare?" Without waiting for an answer the Customs man marked the bags. Then he looked up, a little hesitantly. "Do you have. . .I mean, are any of you carrying. . ."

The gentleman smiled a little and finished the sentence for him. "Any fire arms? Yes, of course, these men are my bodyguards. Gentlemen, the weapons and your permits, please."

At the command, the eight men reached inside their jackets and in unison presented eight small automatics. The U.S. permits were laid on the counter beside the guns. The Customs official examined the serial numbers and the signatures on the permits. Then he handed back the guns, and read:

"Use of these weapons is under the jurisdiction of United States law, and the applicable law of the State of Florida. Any accusation of illegal use will be tried by a U.S. District Court. You status as foreign nationals grants you no immunity. . . .This is just a formality, you understand."

The bodyguards nodded, and returned the weapons to their holsters.

Their employer spoke again. "Of course. These weapons are here only to protect me." He bowed, and left quickly, followed by his men.

As the entourage swept out of the lounge, the two officials looked at each other, and sighed.

"Whew! I hope I never have to go through something like that again. Who is that guy, anyway?"

"I sure don't know. Must be a real big shot, though. The word came down, royal treatment, no holds barred."

"Does South Africa have a king? Maybe that's who it was."

"Nope, and the President would have come on a government plane. That's a commercial job out there. Whoever he is, he must be a mighty important man."

Two sleek limousines met the arrivals and swept them into Miami Beach's plushest hotel. An entire floor had been reserved for their use. To compensate for jet-lag, the South African ordered bedrooms darkened, and the men prepared to catch up on sleep. Before retiring, the South African had ordered one of his men to make a phone call.

"Telephone Mr. Winston and advise him that I have arrived. I will see him here, in five hours. You may also order dinner, but Mr. Winston will not be dining with me."

* * *

When Edward Winston arrived at the hotel that evening, the lights of Miami Beach were just beginning to twinkle. His driver pulled up to the entrance, helped him out, then was directed to the subterranean parking garage.

Winston straightened his tie, checked the shine on his shoes, and smoothed down the back of his coat. Pulling himself strictly erect, he entered the hotel. Two of the South African's bodyguards met him, and escorted Winston to the elevator that had been reserved for their exclusive use. They stood silently as the elevator hummed its way to the twenty-second floor. Winston noticed that his hands were trembling.

Leaving the elevator, the proceeded to a door at the end of the hall. One of the guards knocked. They were ordered in.

The tall man was standing with his back to the door, looking out over the ocean, as Winston entered alone. The man turned, holding a drink in his left hand, and gestured to the bar.

"Good evening, Ed. Help yourself to a drink."

"Thank you, sir." Winston poured himself a glass of fine old scotch, then waited expectantly.

"Oh, sorry. Please sit down, Ed. You'll find the chairs in this hotel very comfortable."

"Thank you, sir. I trust everything is well?"

"Quite. Now, tell me about your little Caribbean adventure, Edward."

"Yes, sir. I received a report from my agent that the team has successfully taken a garrison, and have raised quite a bit of support. They will be nearing the capital tomorrow night, as scheduled."

"I see. Well, I've made a few changes, Ed. I will be flying to Port-au-Prince myself tomorrow—to have a little chat with the *Président*. No, no, don't interrupt. I will be perfectly safe. I intend to tell him of this assault on his sovereignty, very tactfully, of course, and suggest that perhaps he would like to, ah, cooperate, with us in the future. What do you think?"

Winston was unable to speak, stunned that the careful plan had been so lightly tossed aside.

"Yes, sir, that should be very effective," he said at last. "Will there be any problem about the agreement with the other parties involved?"

"That? Oh, that's nothing. Those little island dictators are accustomed to people changing their minds. . .no, that *mulatto* will not object. I think I'll bring him with me, in fact."

"Yes, sir. Sir, may I remind you that I have some very good agents involved in this? They are a bit too valuable to throw away."

"Yes, of course, Ed. That is why I am informing you of my plans, so you can make the necessary arrangements. Perhaps you could radio them, and instruct them to leave quickly. Of course, the rebels are not to know. *M'sieur le Président* must have something to catch, something to make him think. Pull out your agents, but leave that rag-tag army for a prize." The man stood, dismissing Winston.

* * *

Leaving the hotel, Winston tried to grasp this jarring change in plans. He ordered his driver to Hunter's hotel. He hoped that Ramirez would be able to radio the team in time. Winston's employer would be very unhappy if there were an actual assault on Port-au-Prince.

27

The foothills of the Haitian coastal range are strangely
lovely at sunset. The last rays of the setting orb light a
golden mist rising from the trees. Purple shadows
appears behind every rock and tree. The lazy buzzing of
insects and the last chirping of tropical birds make a
melancholy chorus. In the distance can be seen the lonely
streamers of smoke from the cook-fires of far-off
settlements. To the south, the bright lights of the great
capital city glimmer faintly against the deepening
twilight.

This evening, on a plateau a thousand feet above the
valley formed by a winding river, a large army of men
made camp for the night. They did not look like an army.
In place of the khaki and boots of soldiers were the
brightly colored garb of *carnaval* pilgrims: fantastic hats,
gourd rattles, and garlands of exotic flowers. If anyone

had seen them, they would have believed that this was a group headed for *Carnaval* in the capital, to do honor to their *Président*.

But they had made their way, recruiting as they went, from Bouli down the ragged trail to La Chappelle, across the Artibonite river, and into the mountains again. By the time they had descended into the foothills again, their numbers were swollen with farmers, merchants, *marrons*, thieves and guerillas. They were now over two hundred strong. This was the force that had assembled here in holiday array, awaiting a signal from their leader.

Tucked deep into the hills was a small group of fighting men, piles of arms and munitions, and a tent, slightly larger and better made than the others. Inside sat the provocateurs, the terrorist team of World Transport. Only one member of the group, their assassin, was missing. It was time for Esteban Ramos to break the radio silence of the past two days, and contact the base in the Dominican Republic. In less than thirty-six hours, Port-au-Prince would erupt in violence.

* * *

Ulysse Follette walked a broken path, skirting men and fires, to where Mama Dimanche was sitting with a group of peasants.

"Ah, there you are, Mama. I would like to talk with you and your men. Since we are so close, we should review once again the battle plan."

"Battle, my friend? Are we not a simple group of *carnaval* goers?" she said playfully.

Follette frowned.

"A jest, Follette," she said. "You are right. Let us go and talk with them."

She rose, excusing herself from the group, and walked with Follette to the large tent. As they approached it from the rear, a low burst of static startled Follette. He glanced sharply at Dimanche.

"A radio, Mama? You did not tell me that your men had a radio."

She thought quickly.

"Yes, Follette. They are checking the government channels to see if any troops are being mobilized near us. Come—we will go away for awhile, and return when they are through."

"No. I would like to hear this." His hand snaked out and grasped her wrist and she began to turn away. Close by the tent wall they listened intently.

" 'Carib' calling. We have successfully completed section three, and are near the goal, over." It was Ramos speaking.

" 'Carib,' Ramirez responded. Signal *Abort*, repeat, *Abort*. You are ordered out. Plan Omega, but repeat, *abort* 'Carib.' Over." There was silence.

"Do you read, 'Carib'?"

"Affirmative. Abort 'Carib'—plan Omega. Out."

Follette turned a dark glare to the woman beside him. He could feel her arm tremble, and saw a look of stunned surprise on her face.

"What. . .?" he began in a harsh whisper. She gestured vehemently for silence, and leaned closer to hear what was being said in the tent.

Inside, Boyette wiped his brow, and looked around at the group.

"Omega, gentlemen," he said. "Ramirez's instructions to be implemented if we were betrayed. It is strange. *I* was to notify *him* if Omega became necessary."

Ramos was furious.

"How could we have been betrayed? How could Ramirez know something we don't? Unless. . .unless it is orders from that man Winston. Could he be double-crossing my General?"

"If it is a double-cross," Cain said thoughtfully, "then somebody is gonna get stomped. I got a feeling that the somebody is that bunch of peasants with us. Otherwise why would Ramirez order us out?"

"Gentlemen," Boyette cut in, "we could speculate all night. The fact is. . .we know nothing, except that we are to get ourselves out quickly, but see that Follette's 'army' goes in on schedule. Let us now consider how we are going to manage it."

"Getting out is simple," interjected Carter. "All you gotta do is get us to the plane, and I'll have you safe and sound in no time."

"We have agreed that Mama Dimanche is expendable, Henri," said Ramos. "I propose we simply find some pretext to separate from her and from Follette's men, and slip away while they take the brunt of the fighting."

Martinez raised his eyebrows, but he did not speak. Ira Cain was furious.

"What you're talking about amounts to murder! She's one of us, Boyette. Throwing her to the *Président*'s wolves is a lousy stinking double cross!"

"Mr. Cain, this woman is a fanatic," said Boyette. "If she knew what we were planning she might do something unpredictable."

The tent flap flew back, and like a raging leopard the woman struck. She was followed by Follette. They were met by wild gunfire. Her iron-hard hands slashed at throats and skulls. Her feet lashed out in defense. Follette fired wildly into the melee. The sound of battle brought the guerillas racing to the tent.

Mama Dimanche turned from where the six terrorists lay. Follette faced her, his gun leveled at her head.

"Thank you for your assistance, Madame. Now, perhaps you will tell me the truth. It seems that there is much that I did not know."

"Before we talk, Follette, may I urge you to bind these men?"

Follette snapped the order to his men. A few of the *marrons* entered, and bent over the men on the ground.

"These two are dead, Ulysse." One of Follette's men gestured to Carter and Ramos. "I don't think the old

196

man will make it. What do you want to do with these two?" He pointed at Boyette and Cain.

"Take them outside, and watch them," Follette answered. "I wish to speak with this woman alone."

The men left the tent, burdened by the bodies of the terrorists. Follette held the gun loosely, but kept it trained on the woman before him.

"And now, Madame, you will explain this 'Carib' to me."

"Follette, I am ashamed." Swiftly and bluntly, she told him everything: how World Transport planned to take over the island, how they were to foment civil unrest to give an excuse for the Dominican army to invade, how he and his men were to be sacrificed.

"But Follette, when I agreed to this plot I did not know what I know now." Her voice grew colder. "I joined these provocateurs for reasons of my own. For some reason, it did not occur to me. . ." She shook her head. "I had not seen the suffering here, I had not heard your dreams for the future."

"You had not seen. . .? But you were *born* on this island! You *must* . . . Who are you?" The gun came again.

She did not reply. Her hands reached up, pulling loose the wild mane of hair. Her fingers moved over her face, changing its contours. Her palms covered her eyes. Where one dark eye had been, there were now two of ice blue. Her chill voice spoke. "*I am Nightshade.*"

She moved slowly closer, looking deep into his eyes. Slowly, he began to lower his gun.

"I am a victim, like yourself, Follette. It has taken this to make me see that in this land I am only one of many. From this moment forward, you struggle is my own. *You must believe me.*"

"Yes," said Follette in a dazed whisper, "yes, I do believe you."

Follette shook his head, as if to clear it. He looked down at the gun in his hand, then stuffed it into his belt. He sighed, his voice full of bitter defeat. "It is finished. Everything is lost."

"No," Nightshade's voice rang out in challenge. "Everything is gained. Now we can go in without threat of intervention and make a *real* revolution in Haiti. The day of retribution has come. The man in the palace has harmed many."

"The soldiers will be waiting for us. You heard that we were betrayed."

"If they are waiting, they will be waiting in the north. Suppose we strike from the east?"

"We could cut them off!"

"Yes, Follette, we can use this betrayal against them."

"Let me think," Follette said. "One moment we are betrayed, the next. . .well, perhaps this adventure may yet succeed, Madame—Nightshade. But what of the poor people who have thrown their lot in with us? I do not wish to lead them into such danger."

"Let us send them home, without shame. We will take with us only the most dedicated, the best fighters. A large army would only slow us, now. For if the *Président* has been informed, he will know the original plan. We must move quickly, surprise him."

"You are wise, Madame. My men have come this far. They will follow me further. Let us speak to the others."

The two left the tent together. Outside, the *marrons* stood in a tight group around the unconscious provocateurs. The peasants stood aside, uncertain of what was happening. Nightshade stayed in the shadow, as Follette spoke. "My friends," his voice rang out, "my friends, I have grave news—there are traitors in our ranks!"

A moan went up from the assembled crowd, followed by a low murmur of fear. Follette quieted them with a raised hand.

"These men before you would have betrayed you to the desires of a powerful man across the border." This time the reaction was anger. "Peace. Peace, my brothers, it is not our way to circumvent justice. The traitors will be taken care of, in time. But listen to me. Although we cannot hope to take the city with the mighty army as we had planned, there is still a small chance that our cause will be fruitful. I need your help.

"I know that many of you must be fearful. Many of you have families to think of. I would not be truthful if I did not say that many of you who come with me may die tomorrow, or that the risk of treachery is not yet great. Those few among you who would dare this enterprise I welcome with a heart full of gratitude. Those of you who fear, who would return to your homes and families, go now, without blame, and with my friendship. I am grateful that you have followed me for so long."

As Follette's words died, a moving scene unfolded in the encampment before him. Many of the men were talking actively, some were deep in thought. His words had struck deep, and each man was making a decision that could affect the rest of his life.

Gradually the murmur subsided. Some men went to pack their few possessions, preparing to leave. Others came to stand before their leader. In a few minutes less than one hundred men remained of the great band of *carnaval* goers, their faces proud and hard. Most of them were the hill guerillas who had fallen in with them in the beginning, but a few peasants, such as young Roger Fournier, stood in the group before Follette, their eyes filled with his dream.

"Thank you, my friends," said Follette, his voice filled with emotion, "thank you for your faith in me. If we are strong, and trust in one another, we can yet prevail. The time is ripe. By tomorrow night, Haiti will be ours!" A great cheer, as one voice, answered him.

* * *

Boyette first, and later Cain, came to consciousness during the speech. Boyette, wrists bound, struggled to his feet. Several men closed around him.

"Get back!" he shouted. "I wish to speak with Follette." Warily, they escorted him to the rise where Follette stood.

"Ulysee Follette, I wish to speak to you."

"I will no longer listen to the lies of traitors, Boyette."

"And what of the woman who betrayed us to you? You will trust her not to betray you as well?"

Follette gestured to the shadows. His men watched intently as Nightshade stepped from the darkness. Her glacial eyes glinted in the twilight, and her long raven hair hung about her shoulders. For a moment Boyette could only stare at this transformed woman, then he challenged her.

"This woman is an impostor! She is not who she claims to be! The witch, Mama Dimanche, is dead!"

Nightshade glanced at the peasants who crowded around her.

"You are only half right, Boyette. Indeed, Mama Dimanche is dead. . ." She clapped her hands together and produced a leaping flame. ". . .but the *witch* remains!" The flames licked out and singed Boyette's face. He fell to his knees.

Nightshade's mirthless laugh rang out, and with a flourish, the fire was gone. Many of the guerillas crossed themselves.

Follette spoke again. "This woman who called herself Mama Dimanche is a powerful ally, a *bocur* called Nightshade. She will help to guide our plans to success. And now we must decide what to do with these wolves in our midst."

Boyette still sat crouched on the ground. A short distance away the still form of Manuel Martinez ebbed its life away. Ira Cain, bound, came forward.

"M'sieur Follette, I have nothing to offer, and no way to prove that what I say is true, but I do have something to say. You are planning to try and take the city without experts like Boyette, Ramos and Martinez to help you, and chances are you're gonna fail. But there is a chance you could make it, *if* you can get to the *Président* in time. I would like to go with you—to help you."

"Traitor!" snapped Boyette.

"Traitor? Maybe, but to who? This is a *black* nation, Boyette, and maybe my first chance to fight *for* people, instead of against them. How about it? You can either kill me now, or accept me. I've got a lot to offer you. I've been doin' this kind of work for the last ten years. If you want me, I'm yours."

Follette looked first at Cain, then turned to Nightshade.

"Well, Madame Nightshade?"

She stepped close to Cain. Eyes filled with cold fire searched his. He trembled.

"Let him come with me. I will be responsible."

"It is done. Release him."

Boyette began to protest.

"As for you, you cunning serpent, I should tread you under my heel, but that is not my way. You will be held here, and released after we have taken the city. . .or died in the attempt. After that, well, I'm sure *someone* will find you. Now get out of my sight."

Boyette was led away.

* * *

Fearing that the *Président*'s men might already be on their way, the guerillas made ready to go as swiftly as they could. They would make their approach tonight, instead of waiting for the morning.

One group was designated to remain in the north, with explosives, ready to blow up the main road behind the *Président*'s troops to prevent them from returning to the city. Other small bands were organized to make assaults on the armories, police station and power plants—the nerve centers of the capital. Nightshade herself would breach the Presidential Palace. Follette would take the Government radio station, to announce the death of the *Président*. It was hoped that many would rally to their side, once the fear of *le Président* no longer gripped them.

At last, at the darkest hour of the night, the attack teams were ready. Ulysse Follette moved among the men speaking words of encouragement. The mood of the group was one of high excitement.

As the night began to ebb, the macabre army, dressed in *carnaval* attire, moved like ghosts toward Port-au-Prince.

28

Carnaval time in Port-au-Prince. Declared periodically by the government, it brought a little life into the terrorized city, drew tourist trade, and gave the current *Président* a time to bask in the forced adulations of his unwilling people. At *carnaval* time, the streets of the City of Contrasts teem with hundreds of revelers, even in the early afternoon. Everywhere are masks, bright colors, noisemakers, flowers. A bottle of rum is raised to the sky, then passed among a hundred neighbors. Dancing, shouting crowds make their way down the wide boulevards in the central city.

Even in the narrow alleys and filthy byways of the slums there is joy. Factories are closed, the people have the day to relax from back-breaking work in strenuous joy. The only people working today are the shopkeepers, the street vendors. They do a steady business in souvenirs for the tourists and food for the natives. The rum-sellers are busy too.

For the soldiers, restraint is the key word this week: Make a bright and happy town to draw in more tourist dollars. Soon they will all go to the private treasury of *M'sieur le Président*.

* * *

A strolling *loup garou* has concealed his gun, and is obvious only by his big dark glasses. A young man lounging by the police station looks up nervously as the dark figure passes, then offers a bottle. The *loup garou* takes it and drinks deep, then walks on, still holding the bottle. The young man sighs. A small price to pay to be left unobserved.

To the north, near the Presidential Palace, a crowd falls suddenly silent, then flurries from the middle of the street. From out of the wide gates of the Palace rolls a convoy of trucks bristling with troops. They speed north, and as the last truck passes, a soldier, ranking high by his uniform, shouts to the crowd: *"Vive M'sieur le Président!* Let him hear the joy of his loving people!"

The crowd breaks its silence to sing, in ragged, nervous voices, a hymn of praise to their leader. As they sing, twenty men, carrying great baskets of flowers, move away from the crowd to follow the convoy at a discreet distance.

To the south, well away from the government buildings, an unusually noisy group of revelers begins chanting. They attract the interest of passers-by, and are joined. The level of shouting rises, and, someone in the crowd begins to chant *"Vive Follette!"*

Hearing the sound of approaching jeeps, the group fades away, leaving nothing but a whispered echo to greet the arriving guard.

A few minutes later, Palace Guards hear the same slogan shouted from a few blocks away. They hurry

toward the noise, to find only an empty square. The chant rises again, to the south.

**

At the government radio center, three young soldiers are lazily making their rounds. The *Président* has personally recalled them from *Carnaval* leave, so there can be little grumbling. As they are about to leave the control room, a call comes through from the troops sent north.

"Calling Headquarters, calling Headquarters ... over."

One of the men hurries to the microphone.

"This is Capital Headquarters. Please report, over."

"This is General Martine speaking. We have reached the site where guerilla action was reported. There are signs that many men were camped here some hours ago, but we have made no sightings. It is urgent that you contact the *Président* at once, over."

"Yes, sir. I will call His Excellency immediately. Over and out."

Suddenly a strange voice speaks from the doorway. "You will not call anyone."

The three soldiers whirl, and see ten men with rifles trained on them. One of the soldiers breaks for the door, and is clubbed down. The intruders advance, and the two remaining soldiers fall.

As Ulysse Follette smiles at his men, raising a clenched fist in a gesture of victory, a faint rumble, like distant thunder, comes from the north.

**

As the deep twilight began to settle on the *Carnaval* city, two men wearing the distinctive white coats, black suits, and dark glasses of the *loups garous* approach the Palace Gates. They are challenged by a single sentry.

"Halt!"

The taller of the two stepped forward.

"His Excellency requested that we report to him when the disturbances in the south were quelled. He ordered us to appear in person."

"I have not heard of any disturbances to the south, to the north, yes, but. . ."

"I am not surprised. His Excellency asked that we subdue the rioters as swiftly and silently as possible, so as not to disturb the tourists."

The soldier was reluctant to disobey the *loups garous*. He waved them through, and stepped out into the street to see if he could locate the source of the riots. When he turned, the two in black were gone.

Once inside the compound, the two looked around them. A handful of the palace guard were lounging about, drinking and singing *carnaval* songs. They tensed, coming to lax attention as the two *loups garous* passed. As the two crossed to the great white door which marked the entrance to the palace, a neatly-dressed officer came running up at a trot.

"It's Follette! He has returned! Some of my men saw him near the Iron Market. There is talk he is planning to lead a march on the palace!"

As the young officer came close to the *loups garous*, he was struck viciously across the face by a white glove. He reached for his gun, but two submachine guns turned toward him.

"You stupid, cowardly fool!" the *loup garou* cursed him. "There is a riot in the Iron Market, and your men stand around here drinking? If Follette has returned, you must go and find him! Get out of my sight—and take every able-bodied man you can find with you, drunk or sober. Follette must not be allowed to escape!"

Stunned, the officer quickly rounded up his men, and soon they were piling into an old jeep.

The man in black shouted. "Go! What are you waiting for! I will notify His Excellency. Now go!"

The jeep made a hasty departure. The *loups garous* knocked at the palace door. A man opened it, and challenged them to produce identity cards. The taller figure forced past, announcing, "Cocoyé! Your *Président*'s life is in danger! Let me by!"

The bewildered guard, unwilling to risk his career, fell back. The two strode quickly forward, coming at last to a long hall.

The leader gestured to a stairway at the far end. "That way leads to the basement where the arms are stored, Cain. Nearby you should find the generator. You know what to do. I'm going upstairs to find *M'sieur le Président*!"

Ira Cain paused for a moment at the top of the stairs.

"Look, whoever you really are, I—I want to thank you for taking a chance on me—"

Nightshade cut him off. "There's no time for that now."

Cain's face twisted in a half smile. "Okay, whatever you say. Whichever way it goes, I'll be waiting for you outside in thirty minutes. Oh, and good luck!"

But the woman in black had vanished.

* * *

The Presidential Palace is an island of opulence in a sea of squalor. Built and rebuilt in a crazy combination of Louis XVI and neo-Victorian, it is sumptuously carpeted in red, and the walls are adorned with gilt and marble.

In the room outside the *Président*'s private study, a strange collection of guards stood duty. The two ornately carved wooden doors were closed, and two richly dressed members of the *Président*'s elite guard stood at attention, rifles shouldered.

In two pairs, flanking the Presidential guard on either side, were men in the tan uniforms of the Dominican Military Police. Standing nearby, casually, dressed in immaculate white suits of a fashionable cut, were two tall blond men, almost alike. They were unmoving, as if cut from wax.

The men in white were the first to hear the footfall of the approaching *loup garou*. The wheeled as one, hands moving toward their guns.

A slim man, almost as tall as they, stood before them cradling a machine gun. He wore a black suit and shirt with white tie and gloves, and a loosely belted white trenchcoat. The pale blue eyes of the men in white met the insect glare of his dark glasses.

For a moment, no one spoke. Then the *loup garou* gestured at the door with his gun, and spoke in a thick Creole dialect.

"Tell the *Président* that I have a message for him—and be quick about it. I cannot answer for what will happen if he is not informed."

The two palace guards trembled and turned to unlock the door. One of the men in white turned his gun on the guards, while the other kept the intruders under cover.

"There were explicit instructions that the *Président*, General Cruz and his guest were not to be disturbed for any reason." The man in white spoke in faintly accented French.

The palace guard stopped, helpless.

"I am sorry, M'sieur. I can do nothing. It—it is the order of His Excellency *M'sieur le Président* himself!"

The *loup garou* wheeled and left without a word. The Dominican soldiers looked at the guard quizzically. The men in white followed the intruder with their eyes. When at last the sound of the footsteps faded, the men in white resumed their waxen posture.

29

Three men sat in the book-lined study.

Seated erect in a comfortable chair, a handsome man with a broken nose and coffee-colored skin toyed with the brass buttons on his tan uniform. The heat was oppressive tonight, even with the casement opened to admit the breeze, and he ran a finger under his shirt collar. He did not speak.

Across from him, behind a great mahogany desk that almost dwarfed him, was a small, stout black man in a plain dark suit. In his late thirties, he wore a pair of thick steel wire-rimmed glasses. His big hands were folded in front of him, but in constant motion, and his head would cock itself suddenly from time to time in odd attitudes. He was also silent.

The third man lounged casually in a great red leather easy chair, a cigar smoldering in a fine crystal ashtray, an excellent brandy in his hand. He wore a loose-fitting linen suit that emphasized his massive, muscular frame. His graying hair was in contrast to his tanned skin. His face was lean and finely chiseled. He spoke now, in English, slowly and easily, in a rich, Oxford-educated voice.

"So you see, my dear Mr. President, I have a great deal to offer you. You shall never want for funds, you shall have the whole of my organization behind you, and if I may put it this way, you will be joining the wave of the future. You have had one demonstration today of what can be accomplished with my cooperation and aid. Think of the possibilities for the future.

"Your *cooperation*?" The small man peered owlishly through his spectacles. "You come to me with warnings of a band of lunatics, which you yourself may have set at my throat. You play your left hand against your right to catch me in between. You call this cooperation?"

"My dear Mr. President," the South African's voice was honey-sweet, "surely a man such as yourself, a man of certain. . .political experience, can understand the value of a little display. After all, no harm has been dône. . .in fact, I would remind you that I have actually donè you a service. You might never have captured those 'lunatics' if it had not been for my cooperation."

The *Président* raised his head. "It is all very well for you to speak thus, M'sieur. I am a patient man, and will listen to anything I believe will help my country and my people." The Dominican General cast a cold glance at him, but he continued, unheeding. "But you are promising things no one man, no, not even the President of the United States, could guarantee. Despite what you know about plans to kill me, despite these gestures of good faith, despite the generous loans you have offered me to do business with you, I am yet not convinced."

Here the *Président* paused to light a cigar of his own. He drew on it several times, seeming entranced with the patterns the smoke made in the air. In the silence, they could hear the sounds of *Carnaval* floating in the window with a welcome breeze.

"You hear that, M'sieur? That is wealth to me. The sound of my people, happy, dancing, celebrating their beloved *Président*. What can you offer me that can rival this, the adulation of my people?" A great shout arose as he spoke.

The *Président* pointed with his cigar at General Cruz.

"Tell me, Moses, my old enemy, what has this pale-skinned foreigner offered you which makes you so wholly his slave?" He smiled as he savored the word.

Cruz barely restrained his anger. The South African's lips narrowed, but otherwise he betrayed no sign of anger.

Cruz replied, "Under the hand of this man, my country is enjoying a prosperity we never dreamed of before. You speak of your people, and their love for you. They have starved for so long, they would go over without a moment's hesitation to one such as this Follette who throws them a crust of bread—if only your werewolves did not come and take away in the night any who dare speak against their 'beloved *Président*'. Do you not realize that if you will only do business with this gentleman, you will have all the same luxuries you now enjoy, and this island as a whole will again become a pearl of the Caribbean?"

"And what if I refuse your generous offer and say 'I am very well by myself thank you'?"

The South African leaned forward. "I'm afraid that's impossible."

"What do you mean 'impossible'? Nothing is impossible for me, I am the *Président*. I am—"

But the sentence was never finished. As the *Président* spoke, the lights failed and the three men sat in darkness. Cruz rose suddenly, and the South African pulled himself erect. The *Président* began to mumble something about a power failure, but Cruz cut him off.

"*Listen!*"

There was no sound, only an uncanny silence for the first time in four days and four nights. Then, quietly at first, then building to an awesome volume, came a great rattle from the east, as if a thousand skeletons were dancing the *Carnaval* dance.

"*Tonnère!*" the *Président* swore, "it is the *tènèbres!*"

It had been over a decade since the *tènèbres* or "shadow protest" had been heard in the city. It was the sound of hundreds, thousands of people tapping on light poles, trash cans, automobiles, anything that would make a noise. The *Président* himself had organized such protests during the long years of his own fight for power. It was said that the *tènèbres* had the power to liberate the *loa bossals*, the wild spirits that fought for possession of one's body. The *Président* moved back, as if trying to disappear into the wall behind him.

There was a great explosion outside the window, and the light from it glinted on the beads of sweat on the *Président's* face.

Cruz swore. "Follette and his men—they have escaped! We must alert the guards! They will be here soon!"

Cruz began to cross to the ornate telephone in front of the terrified *Président*. He was held motionless by a cold, inhuman voice.

"*Do not move or you die!*"

Standing by the opened window stood a tall dark woman with gleaming ice-blue eyes and raven hair. She was dressed in black. A machine gun rested easily in her hand.

The *Président* turned to her, his great white eyes gaping behind the steel frames. "How did you get here? Who are you? *What* are you?"

The woman's icy voice held them motionless.

"I am Fate. I am your Nemesis. I am the hand of Justice finally reaching out to weigh you. I am your

Death, M'sieur—but you may call me *Nightshade*."

The *Président* began to babble in a whisper to himself, a trickle of spittle drooling down his lips, as if convulsed in a *petit mal* seizure. Cruz was unable to move.

The South African took a step forward, his poise unshaken.

"What do you want?"

"I have come for Justice, as I have said. Don't you recognize me?"

The South African shook his head slowly.

"I am every man, woman and child whose life was forfeited to make your 'wave of the future.' I am the broken and twisted human carnage upon which you have raised your white and pristine empire. It is ones such as I from whom you have drawn your strength—*and it is I who have been chosen to take it from you*."

The South African nodded slowly in comprehension. He looked at her carefully, his eyes at last coming to rest on hers, ice for ice.

"So—my old Nightmare—you actually exist."

"Yes. You created me. And now your creation has come to destroy you!"

As she raised her gun, the South African pulled the stunned form of Moses Cruz before him, touching a button on his watch. The door flew open, and the men in white entered, guns drawn.

Unsurprised, Nightshade clapped her hands together, and the room was suddenly filled with a blinding light—followed by the sound of gunfire. There was a horrible shriek, and the sound of a body falling to the floor.

* * *

One of the palace guards rushed in to light a candle, stumbling over a fallen figure. In the eerie half-light of the taper, the South African scanned the room. The woman had vanished. The men in white were squeezing

215

off shots out the open window. A moment later, one turned to his master.

"She's gone, sir."

The South African dealt him a vicious blow across the face that drove him to his knees. He rose slowly, dabbing the trickle of blood at the corner of his mouth with a neatly-folded handkerchief.

On the floor before the South African, Moses Cruz lay on his back, a single bullet through his skull. Behind the great wooden desk, its surface chopped by machine gun fire, lay the still form of the *Président*. The palace guard knelt over him. A great bloody hole was ripped through the arm and shoulder of his coat.

The *Président* lifted his head, turning a maniacal glare on the South African.

"Get out! Get out, you! You bring Death to the *Président*! You should know that the *Président* cannot be killed! Get out before I have your head cut off and hung in the city square! Go!"

The South African dusted his suit, as if soiled by the madman's words. As the *Président* reached for his telephone, the South African left the room without looking back.

30

Nightshade ran, swift as a jungle cat through the darkness. Reaching the high wall of the Palace compound, she vaulted up, her claws scrabbling for a hold on the sheer stone wall. Then she was over and dropping to the ground below.

Ira Cain whirled, about to fire, then stopped. "Is it done? Is he dead?"

She said nothing, and Cain knew that the *Président* still lived. She began to run again, and Cain followed after her, limping slightly from the pain of his ankle, aggravated by his own escape.

The moved from shadow to shadow around to the front of the palace, swarming with guards and *loups garous* summoned by the President's call. Cain, still wearing his trenchcoat, pulled glasses from his pocket. Nightshade swiftly overpowered a passing *loup garou*, took his coat and dark glasses, and stuffed her luxuriant hair into the dark hat with the white band. Running forward, she gestured to a chauffeur waiting by a car with a Presidential seal on the door.

"You! Out of the way! One of the assassins has escaped!" Without waiting for an answer, she and Cain forced their way into the limousine, and squealed out of the driveway, bursting through a lowered gate. In the glare of the powerful headlights, Nightshade could see the soldiers leaping out of the way.

Once on the main street, she turned on the wailing siren and leaned repeatedly on the horn. Cain was astonished at first.

"Why the hell are you doing that?"

She turned to look at him as if aware of his presence for the first time.

"This is no time to be cautious. We have only minutes to save the lives of Follette and his men. With the forces of the *Président* alerted, no one who even whispers of revolution will be safe within the hour." She continued more softly, "If Follette is taken, I will be to blame. I only hope we reach him in time."

* * *

Nothing would have surprised the peasant on the streets of Port-au-Prince that night. First, it was *carnaval*, a time when traditionally anything can happen. Second, there had been rumors of riot and revolution all day, and threats of fierce reprisal. And now it was nighttime, when all the spirits of the dead were at large, and strange things could happen.

But for one peasant, strolling drunkenly home from a night of dancing and carousing, there were more surprises in store. As he passed before the great white facade of the Government Radio Network building, he was challenged by a fierce-looking man in peasant's rags and a *carnaval* hat, holding a rifle.

He shook his head to shake the vision away, but it persisted. He swore he would never drink so much *clairin* again, at least at one time, but he put his hands up, just in case the vision was real.

As he began to protest his innocence and beg to be allowed to go home and sleep it off, he heard far off the wail of the siren of a government car. The reveller with the gun turned toward the sound, and the peasant turned to run, knowing, from long experience, better than to be caught in such a conflict.

Around the corner wheeled a great black limousine, with two of the dreaded *loups garous* behind the wheel. It swung in an arc, coming up over the curb between the peasant and the man with the gun. The two werewolves got out.

"Where's Follette?"

The gunman raised his weapon to fire. Then, to the peasant's astonishment, the *loup garou* shed the trenchcoat and hat. It was a woman! The peasant fled into the night, offering silent entreaties to his gods for deliverance from this night of madness.

* * *

Nightshade passed the sentry with Cain, now shedding his own coat. They were given passage by the guerillas on duty to the small studio with burlap-covered walls where Follette waited to address the people. From the studio monitors came the sound of a lively instrumental tune with an island rhythm. A graying guerilla stood by a small transmitter waiting for the signal from the palace that the *Président* was dead. As he looked up, Nightshade entered.

"Where is Follette?"

"In there." Nightshade came to a smaller room, where Follette sat before a microphone, working on a sheaf of white paper before him. He glanced up to see the dark woman enter.

221

"I have failed you, Ulysse, your revolution is over. The *Président* yet lives, and will be sending his war machine against you." Nightshade's icy calm nearly broke. "Come, let us get away, now, while there is time!"

Follette leaned back, a great weight of weariness settling on his shoulders. His brow furrowed deeply in thought, then he looked up in resolution.

"My revolution has only begun, Madame. Perhaps this battle will be lost, but the struggle will continue." He signalled to the engineer in the other studio through the glass window. The engineer adjusted several controls, and a red bulb lit up before him.

Nightshade tried once more.

"Please, Ulysse. You must get away while there is still time. The people need you!"

"How could I leave now, and allow hundreds of my people to be slain? No, I have one more thing to do here before I return again to the hills. You must not stay. It is not your fight. . .you must live to wage a greater war than my little battle here. *Adieu, cheri.* The hills will long remember the tale of Nightshade, the woman who lived twice." The music came to an end. Follette looked up again, with the sad smile of a man who has seen too much bloodshed.

"Go now. Before it is too late."

* * *

The limousine hurtled through the night, its wipers beating against the rain which had come with the darkness. The two passengers listened in silence to the government radio station:

"Tonight, my people, we came near to what has not been accomplished in many years—the overthrow of the monster who sits in the Presidental Palace. We have not succeeded this time, but we have proved that nothing can stop us when the time is right.

"Even now, the *Président* summons his *loups garou*s to

rout us. But when they come to find us, we will be gone, like the shadows that fade with the dawn. We will not rest until the enemies of freedom are. . ."

There was a burst of gunfire over the radio. For a moment there was silence, then Follette's voice returned.

"Once again, my friends, they have come to find us. Let us all return to the shadows, to make our battle plans for another day. *Vive Haiti, Vive la Revolution*!" There was another burst of fire, and the station went dead. Cain swore bitterly.

"I don't care what he called himself—Communist, Anarchist, or whatever. He was brave enough to stand up on his two hind legs for what he believed in. I call that a *man*. If only he could have lived to bring about his revolution. . ."

"He may yet live, Ira Cain. It is very hard to kill a dream."

The limousine sped along a new stretch of highway to the southeast that skirted the edge of the posh Petionville suburbs where the ruling class of Port-au-Prince made their homes. There had been no sign of pursuit for many minutes, and the sleek, powerful bulletproof car had been designed with this sort of thing in mind. To the south, the mountains behind Petionville could be made out against the deep blue of the sky. Nightshade sat rigid behind the wheel, the accelerator to the floor, unwilling to slacken her pace.

The new paving gave out a short distance into the hill country. The car began to bounce at the breakneck speed, and Nightshade was forced to go slower to maintain control. As they curved around a great bend in the road, Cain touched her arm.

"What's that up ahead?"

Nightshade peered through the rain with her keen eyes to find what Cain had spotted. When she had made it out, she pushed the accelerator back down to the floor.

A roadblock had been set up across a narrow defile.

"They must've radioed ahead," Cain said.

The shaking was not entirely damped by the expensive suspension of the car. Nightshade's knuckles went white as she gripped the steering wheel. Suddenly it was upon them and she wheeled the car up the side of the embankment, knocking a motorcycle out of the way. It cracked the windshield as it flew past. Just as suddenly, they were beyond it.

But their pursuers were not to be left behind. A convoy of jeeps, cycles and state cars followed as soon as they could reach the road, those in the lead firing shots at glass and tires, even though they knew it was futile.

Since the fugitive's only hope lay in reaching the plane which had been prepared for them, there was no point in taking evasive action. They would have to outrun the pursuit.

Cain twisted the dial of the radio, trying to find the police band. He listened intently to the cryptic communications, but could not make them out.

"What are they saying?"

Nightshade's voice was cold. "They've figured out where we're heading, but not why. They're sending up reinforcements from the south."

"How much further?"

"Perhaps two miles."

"Will we make it?"

"I don't know."

* * *

At over one hundred twenty miles per hour, in the driving rain, on a bad road, with a cracked windshield, it was a miracle that they noticed the mailbox which indicated the side road. Heedless of the dirt track, Nightshade cornered, smashing through the wooden fence, and drove at top speed across the fallow field. The headlights picked out the shape of an old white barn with one side caving in. The car swung in back of it raising a great spray of mud and debris as Nightshade braked to a stop.

The rain was coming in torrents. It was hard to breathe. They ran into the barn where a sleek twin-engine plane was parked, facing the barn door.

"You know how to fly one of these things?" Cain shouted over the sound of the rain on the roof.

"Do you?"

Cain shook his head.

"Then does it matter? I'm going to try the starter. You stay outside and give the propellers a handspin. As soon as they turn over, get into the plane. Don't hesitate, whatever I do. Understood?"

Cain nodded.

For several long, heart-stopping seconds, the engines refused to turn over. At last, with a great roar, the props began to spin as Nightshade opened the throttle. Cain vaulted into the seat next to her.

"What now?"

She indicated to him the throttle and the wheel that controlled the landing gear. She quickly explained how to handle the plane on the ground. Then she jumped out of the plane.

Knocking the blocks out from under the tires, she ran to the far side of the barn and shouldered a great metal drum. She braced herself on one of the wheel struts, and shouted for Cain to start the plane moving.

* * *

As the convoy of Haitian army regulars sped along the road, they found the gaping hole in the fence and turned in to the deserted farm. Two jeeps led the pack.

As they hurtled toward the barn, a twin-engined plane came barreling out of the door, heading directly for them. One jeep swerved aside, the other jeep wheeled around, trying to block the way.

As the plane came nearer, the driver of the jeep saw the wild-eyed face of a she-devil clinging to the wheel strut with one hand, and heaving a great metal can with the other.

As the can struck the jeep, it burst into flames, spewing fuel over the men. They dove from the vehicle just as it exploded.

As if one, the remainder of the convoy swung into an improvised barricade. Nightshade swung into the cockpit, and wheeled the plane about, gunning the motor. The jeeps closed in pursuit.

Cain held tight to the steering column as the plane bumped over the rough ground. Ahead was a low line of trees. He was silently praying for the nose to come up.

At the last moment, the plane turned again in a tight circle driving directly between a pair of jeeps. They began to fire at the disappearing plane as they struggled to turn their vehicles.

A bullet whined through the cockpit from the rear, and Ira Cain whistled low.

"Let's hope the fuel lines are still intact," said Nightshade. As she spoke, the wheels lifted off the ground.

"We've made it, Mama! Halleluja! So long, suckers! If I never see you again it will be too soon."

Nightshade spoke quietly. "I wouldn't be too confident, Cain. We still have to avoid the combined Haitian and Dominican air forces."

As the Haitian soldiers watched, shaking their fists in rage, the little plane vanished into the ebony sky.

31

A tall man with graying hair sat in Edward Winston's custom-made executive chair beside the great plate-glass wall that looked out on the teeming life of the city of New York. Across the desk, Winston sat in a straight-backed chair, his hands folded, his face pale. The South African was slowly shaking his head.

"Edward. Edward, what am I to do with you?" He looked at the man before him as if he were an insect viewed through a microscope.

The South African rose, turning his back on Winston, looking out the window. He spoke quietly, but loud enough for Winston to hear.

"I always take into consideration human frailty, Edward. I expect it in the people I have to rely on. When you are dealing with little men, you can tolerate little mistakes. But you, Edward. I had such hopes for you." He turned quickly. "What were you before I found you?"

"Nothing, sir." Winston's voice faltered.

"*Who* were you?"

"No one, sir."

"Exactly. I made you from nothing and I can return you to nothing. Tell me, Edward, are you afraid of dying?"

"A little, sir." Winston felt like the victim of a cruel little boy.

"I beg your pardon?" The tall man seemed to loom taller.

"No, sir."

A terrible smile crossed the South African's face as he said, "You must realize, Edward, that there are things much worse than death."

Winston felt a wave of sheer terror. He suppressed it.

"It was *she* who was responsible—that Unknown Factor I had always suspected . . . it—she—was real." The South African's gaze came again to Winston, and his nostrils flared.

"And it was *you* who brought her into it. You realize, Edward, that this has ruined all my delicate negotiations. It will take *months* to rebuild them. These petty terrorists are unreliable, and their own feelings get in the way of an efficient performance of their jobs."

The South African shook his head again. "Poor, poor, Edward. What shall I do with you?"

Winston devoutly hoped he would never learn the answer to that question.

32

The curtain rang down to thunderous applause.

As Doctor Black stepped down from the stage, Clara Weiss met her, smiling broadly. "You were magnificent, dear. I thought that the adventure might affect your ability to perform."

"You shouldn't have worried, Clara. Besides, there was opportunity for far more practice than I expected."

"I know. How are you feeling?"

"I'm fine now. Just a little tired. Let's go home."

As the two women walked toward the stage exit, a young man entered with an envelope.

"Doctor Black? This just came for you."

The magician inclined her head to her companion. "Please open it, Clara."

The older woman carefully opened the envelope,

withdrawing a card. She read it intently, and her face clouded.

The younger woman questioned the expression. "What is it, Clara?

Slowly and reluctantly, Clara Weiss handed her the envelope. The paper was rich and heavy, a dull gray. The card was edged with a thick border of silver, like a formal notice of death. In silver ink was written:

Mr. John V. Grey
requests that you honor
an informal gathering of his friends
with a weekend of magic
at his estate in Capetown,
Republic of South Africa
three weeks from date of receipt.
All expenses paid.

RSVP   **BLACK TIE**

AFTERWORD/

Nightshade wasn't created—she was <u>invoked</u>.

It was as if she had always existed, and we had merely conjured her there among us.

It began a couple of years ago. We were at the apartment of Mark Arnold, preparing the syllabus for a course in popular art at Antioch College, when Mark raised the question:

—Doc Savage and The Shadow embodied the spirit of the 1930s. What sort of character would represent the spirit of the 1970s?

The exercise intrigued us. We began to shape such a character deliberately. We wanted him to have the mystery of The Shadow and the cold perfection of Doc Savage. And, knowing that Walter B. Gibson, creator of The Shadow, had a lifelong interest in stage magic, we decided to make him a stage magician. Somebody said ''black''—somebody said ''doctor''—and Doctor Black was born.

He was tall and slim, pale and coldly mysterious, a master of a thousand faces. He was an Avenger, a Nemesis, he was—

A woman.

At which point, we completely lost control of her. It was no longer a question of what we wanted, but of what <u>she</u> wanted. Her origin came first. She had survived attempted destruction, and had vowed revenge on her destroyer, like a long and distinguished lineage of champions (including Edmund Dantes, Don Diego Vega, Bruce Wayne and Gully Foyle).

Over the next year, we began to sketch out a novel about her. While we were in the process of polishing it, along came <u>Weird Heroes</u>. Byron Preiss, with his finger squarely on the pulse of the fantasy-reading public, announced plans for a series of ''New American Pulp Heroes'' in illustrated format. Summoning our gumption, we presented Doctor Black to him.

We had some hesitancy at first. Would a major publisher be willing to take a chance on a heroine who was not frilly, coy or emptyheaded? To our surprise, Byron was enthusiastic about the idea.

To be sure, he had a few strong criticisms. To begin with, Byron had already commissioned veteran s/f editor and writer Ted White to do a modern-day equivalent of Doc Savage, called, appropriately enough, ''Doc Phoenix.'' (His adventures are chronicled in <u>Weird Heroes 2</u>, and soon in his own full-length novel.) Obviously, there couldn't be a spate of ''Doc's'' running around. He asked us to suggest an alternate name for our character.

Again, some Muse was with us as she metamorphosed into <u>Nightshade</u>. The name itself was interesting. First, of course, it hinted at the dark mysteriousness of The Shadow. But it was also the <u>deadly</u> nightshade, source of belladonna—itself an Italian term for a beautiful but deadly woman. And, to play a moment longer, the chemical derived from the poison belladonna is atropine, named for <u>Atropos</u>, the Destroyer, one of the three Fates of Greek myth. So, as well as belonging to the modern pulp tradition, she is born of an older one, with its roots in prehistory. The name change helped bring out the character's most interesting quality—her dual personality.

But, more important, Byron expressed his

very strong feelings about what for want of a better word could be called <u>karma</u>. In creating a series in tune with the 70s, Byron had hoped to show that we had learned something from the turbulent sixties about believing violence can solve our problems. Although he did not wish to tamper with the justified motivation of the character, he asked us to consider the effects of her actions on herself and others. This new theme added, we feel, a new dimension to the character—a conflict between her desire for her revenge, and her desire for justice.

We tried to do one more thing with <u>Terror, Inc</u>. In telling a story about the abuses possible when multinationals and terrorists join forces, we wanted to create a sort of "counter-novel" to the kiss-and-kill men's action series. In the present work, as is often the case in real life, the "good guys" and the "bad guys" change hats. And, surprisingly, history and fiction seem to be on a collision course. The revelations of Watergate and the excesses of the world intelligence community are far more bizarre than anything we have conjectured here. And no amount of plot contrivance could rival the absurdly sinister events in Africa of the past year.

Still, this book is intended primarily as escape, as wish-fulfillment, as entertainment. It's exciting to think of readers identifying with Nightshade in the same way that young readers in the Depression skulked with The Shadow or dared with Doc Savage. If Nightshade succeeds in kindling that spark in some young imagination, she will have done her job.

BETH MEACHAM
TAPPAN KING
New York, 1976

BETH MEACHAM currently works as Conference Coordinator for AFS International Scholarships, a foreign exchange program. She was born and raised in Newark, Ohio, and attended Antioch College in Yellow Springs. While at Antioch, she became involved in writing and producing radio drama, and spent some time as the school's "Pet Coordinator," (a glorified title for dog-catcher.) Ms. Meacham now lives in New York, and writes for the <u>Science Fiction Review Monthly</u> and contributes articles to several semi-pro publications. <u>Nightshade</u> is her first published work of fiction.

TAPPAN KING holds a degree in Communications from Antioch College. At Antioch, he wrote and edited for a number of college publications (including <u>Vomix!</u>, Antioch's legendary underground comic,) and taught a course in Popular Art and Narrative Graphics. Mr. King's work has appeared in a number of publications including the <u>Harvard Journal of Pictorial Fiction,</u> <u>Ariel</u>, and the <u>Science Fiction Review.</u> Mr. King works as a Public Relations writer for The New York Public Library.

MARK ARNOLD lives in—<u>actually lives in</u>—a science fiction bookstore in Yellow Springs, Ohio. Radio drama producer, Clarion Workshop alumnus, and former free-lance columnist for the New York <u>Daily News</u>, his finest literary moment was ghost-writing student term papers while an alcoholic in New Orleans. Mr. Arnold teaches courses in science fiction and the comics at Antioch College, (from which he has not yet graduated).

WEIRD HEROES

A NEW AMERICAN PULP! ™

FICTION *Illustrated*

AMERICA'S FIRST
GRAPHIC NOVEL REVUE

AVAILABLE

WEIRD HEROES
Volume 1: Farmer, Steranko
Lieber, Goodwin $1.50
Volume 2: Farmer, Maggin,
White, Maroto $1.50
Volume 3: QUEST OF THE GYPSY
Goulart/Preiss
Alex Nino $1.50
Volume 5: DOC PHOENIX
White/Wolfman
Fabian—Jan. '77 .... $1.50

FICTION ILLUSTRATED
Volume 1: Schlomo Raven
Detective Comedy $1.00
Volume 2: Starfawn
SF/Star Trek style $1.00
Volume 3: Chandler/Steranko
Deluxe Trade Edition $4.95
Digest Edition $1.00
Volume 4: Son of Sherlock Holmes
Preiss/Reese
Deluxe Trade Edition $4.95
Digest Edition $1.00

Books may be ordered directly from: Pyramid Books, Mail Order, 757 Third Avenue, N.Y. 10017. Orders under $5.00, please add 25¢ per title.

240